For the late, great Louis L'Amour, the master,
who encouraged me to take up Western writing
and bought me a very good lunch.

ONE

The wind coming down from the tree-covered lower slopes behind him whipped up the dust and blew it in Carnigan's face, where it stuck and irritated.

Carnigan wiped his neck with a bandanna already soaked in his own sweat and blew a drop off the end of his nose. It fell on the rock in front of his face and vanished instantly.

Up there, the weather would be cooler and the scent of the trees would be soothing and aromatic in his nostrils. Down here, the wind was hot and quirky, funnelled by the canyon behind him.

He shifted his ground again, and peered between two rocks down on to the trail. A dust-devil raised by a gust of wind whirled past the body of his horse, and vanished into a little cloud of dust before collapsing entirely. Otherwise the scene was one of total desolation.

'Damn,' he said softly to himself. He had been fond of that horse. It was a hammer-headed gelding with a temper like a bear with a hangover, but it had spirit and power and it would go all day on a hatful of water and a scrap of grass which would not keep a mountain sheep alive.

He shifted the pebble he was sucking to keep his mouth moist, and peered again between the boulders.

From this new vantage point, he could have sworn he could see one of them. Something . . . a knee perhaps, at the base of the rock over there.

He sighted the Henry on the knee, breathed out half-way and squeezed the trigger and the stock evenly. The rifle jumped in his hand, and he rolled over once, twice, three times, back to his original loop-hole.

He was just in time to see another Indian leap from his place of concealment, run two paces and dive for a rock just a little nearer to his fort in the rocks.

As the Ute disappeared, a second Indian came out of the dust where Carnigan would have sworn there was not cover enough for a prairie dog, and started his dash forward.

Carnigan nailed him through the middle as he reached full height, and the Ute went down in a puff of dust. There was a chorus of angry yells, and two bullets whined off the rock like hysterical bees.

That would be the two younger men, with their war paint freshly on. The others were too experienced to waste ammunition on a hole in the rock. Bullets were hard to come by out here, and an Indian had to buy them with blood.

Just my luck, he told himself unhappily. Half-way back to the valley in the mountains, supplies secured, pursuers thrown off his trail. And now I'm up to the neck in goddamn Utes.

The shadows were longer than they had been, and the sun was no longer burning down on the back of his neck. Soon it would be dusk. They would come then, when the shapes of the rocks were beginning to go liquid in the failing light, and the silent figures were not so sharp against the land.

He replaced the bullets he had fired from the Henry, and checked that the thong was off the hammer of the Smith & Wesson. He would need every second once they came.

He had never seen the Indians at all. One moment he was riding towards the gateway to the mountains, the next he was running, rifle in hand, for the cover of the rocks.

There was a hole in the flat black hat where one bullet had come entirely too close. And his canteen was out there on the dead horse. The Indians had shot a hole in it to while away the time.

Another drop of sweat had formed on the end of his nose. He blew it off and watched it vanish on the hot rocks. About a half hour, he reckoned, thirty minutes, and they would come.

He rolled again, peering between rocks, but there was nothing to be seen. When they came they would suddenly just be there, where there was no cover, running silently, coming in alternate dashes towards the little knoll with its coronet of rocks which was his fort.

He sucked again at the pebble and tried not to think of coffee. There was no point in lighting a cigarette, since his mouth was already so dry. He felt even a little sleepy.

The Indian was within the circle of rocks with him before Carnigan had even realized he was on the move. His face was strangely impassive as he reached forward with one hand, the axe already swinging in the other.

Carnigan dropped the rifle and rolled desperately, the pistol coming into his hand without conscious thought, the shots ringing in his ears. A hole appeared between the Ute's eyes and he went down as though somebody had cut his strings.

Then they were coming from every direction. No yells, just the silent, running figures, bare legs pumping, rifles held high, coming to kill him.

Carnigan fired like a machine, moving his sights from one target to the next as he worked the lever, not waiting to see the Indians fall. He hit three, and then they were gone.

In the failing sunlight, two bodies lay face down. Where the third had been, there was a dark patch in the dust. Either he had crawled away or one of his comrades had pulled him out of sight.

The shadows deepened and the silence lengthened. However many there had been, they had now lost four dead and one at least badly wounded. It was a high price to pay for a hank of hair and a dead horse. Maybe they would go away. The Indians were as good at adding up the price of their battles as a white man would be, and this had been an expensive battle for them.

He rolled over again, and peered round a rock on the other side of his little enclosure. No living thing was to be seen.

Already it was too dark to make out the outline of his horse with any certainty. If they were coming, they would come now.

He lay where he was, nerves screwed up tighter than he cared to admit, for another quarter of an hour, by which time it was full dark.

Then, an inch at a time, with infinite care, he made his way between the boulders and along the foot of the cliff behind, through the treacherous talus of the slope, until he was within the mouth of the canyon itself.

Nothing moved. No shrill whoop betrayed him. No bullet came out of the dark. Either the Utes had gone, or he had eluded them.

The canyon was narrow and dark even in daylight. At night it was Stygian.

He made his way up it with infinite care, pausing frequently to listen. No sound broke the silence of the place.

There were creatures here, he knew. About him in the dark, tiny things were going about their nocturnal business.

11

Somewhere in the dark there were kangaroo rats. Tucked into the rocks, living apparently upon nothing, there should be cicadas, save that in this breathing darkness they were silent.

At the thought he stopped and hunkered down for a moment.

The cicadas went silent only as self defence. If there were some in the canyon – and if there were not, the place was unique in his experience – they were silent because alien creatures were passing among them.

He was an alien creature. So were the Indians. He remained where he was for a count of perhaps 500, listening with ears which ached to be rewarded with just one sound. The night gave him back nothing.

Carnigan was not a particularly imaginative man, but he felt the hair on the back of his neck ripple slightly. The silence was unnatural, uncanny.

The temptation to move, to run, to break the tension, was almost irresistible, but Carnigan knew it would be fatal.

He needed to be against a wall. Out here in the open he was menaced from all sides. With his back to the wall he did at least know nothing could come from behind.

He moved one foot at a time, rifle clenched in his right hand, supporting himself partly on the extended fingers of his left, like a stalking baboon. The thought stuck in his mind, and he sniggered mentally.

Back there in India, fighting against a different class of Indian, he had been trapped in a rocky box not unlike this one. Then his friends had arrived with a clatter of hoofs and sabres to bring him out. But those dark immaculate horsemen were half a world away now.

A stone shifted under his questing fingers, and he stopped instantly, waiting for some reaction. There was none.

He felt the loom of the cliff face over him, and fumbled his way thankfully between two larger boulders. One of them was the height of his head, and he put his back to it. There was a space to his left and right, the other rock to his front.

As he waited he became aware of just how tired he was. The ride up from Placerville had been long and hard, and he had dismounted and led the horse over the rough places, heavy-laden as it had been.

Now every bone in him ached to relax and sleep. But sleep was out of the question.

Above him the stars in the night sky were beginning to shine and their silver glow was bringing the canyon to life before his eyes. Now, he thought thankfully, the night would give up to him its secrets, and he would know the worst.

But just as the shapes began to grow in the gloom, he heard the first movement. It was out there on the canyon floor and it was a horse, delicately picking its way along the trail.

He heard the hoofs shift and lift, heard a stone crunch under a hoof. Behind the first horse there was a second and a third.

As the animal passed him he got a whiff of grease and woodsmoke, and heard the creak of leather as the Indian shifted his seat. The man must be wearing leggings, he supposed. Indian horses carried no proper saddle, and the Indians never stole them from white men. Born to horseback, they disdained the cumbersome leather equipment.

Four horses in all went past, and far down in the canyon there came the first dry crackle of the cicadas, starting their night song at last. The Indians must have been back there, listening for him as he had listened for them. Sitting on their mounts in the darkness.

The silence of the insects would have given them their hint that he, too, was in the defile, just as it had warned him of them. What they made of the behaviour of the insects now, he had no idea. But they had gone on past him up towards the mountains, and that was bad enough in itself.

They would stop, somewhere ahead, sure that he could not be ahead of them, knowing he would have to follow on.

Now he needed to follow them closely, tagging on behind, so that when they stopped he could stop too, still in contact with the enemy.

He moved fast and silently, eating up the distance, and paused at the bend to survey the trail ahead. As he did so, the canyon came into sharp white light, and he dropped to the ground, carefully cushioning the rifle with his arm.

The moon washed the rocks and walls of the canyon

as though the whole mountain had been dipped in silver.

Carnigan stood in the shadow of the canyon wall and surveyed the next stretch carefully. He could see now, and the horses' hoofs had left deep depressions in the dust of the trail.

The heat was gone from the rocks and the cold of the night was seeping into the place. He shifted his shoulders under the wool shirt, and remembered the sheepskin coat which had been fastened behind his saddle. Momentarily, he considered going back to his dead horse to collect it and some of his supplies, but he dismissed the thought at birth.

The Indians would have looted his saddle-bags as soon as they realized he had gone. There would be nothing back there worth his journey.

There was also at least one wounded Indian to be accounted for. He doubted if the man he had shot but failed to kill would be able to sit a horse with the silent confidence of the three who had ridden ahead. It would make sense to leave him behind to watch the horse.

Damn! Those were determined varmints, he told himself. Why couldn't they just get a notion into their heads to go home?

It happened, often enough. They would decide the game simply was not worth the candle, and fade away into the landscape. Just Carnigan's luck to tangle with a bunch who stuck to their task.

At any rate they had ridden out of sight. He eased

himself out on to the trail again, and catfooted down the length he could see to the next obstacle. There was only about half a mile of the cleft still to go. Then the upper opening of the canyon led on to a meadow at the foot of the mountains. It was wide and there was grass there, and water – which he desperately needed.

But beyond the meadow rose first the foothills, and then the mountains themselves. And up there was his cabin. And his claim.

If they were not waiting for him at the top of the canyon, maybe they were staking out the water. The Utes were mountain Indians, and they might even be on their way home.

In the kind of heat he had suffered that day a man needed a great deal of water, and Carnigan had none. He could go, he knew, for several days without food – had often done so.

But water he must have and soon.

In the real desert there was always some chance of finding a barrel cactus. The pulp of the chubby little plant contained moisture, and it was possible to cut off the top and squeeze the juice out.

But the canyon was not desert. Just a rock-cleft in the barrier between the lowlands and the mountains. From time to time a scrubby, tenacious bush or stunted tree might grow here, and he could see some in the cracks in the walls. But not life-giving cactus.

He would have to get to the water, which was at least half a day's march beyond the head of the canyon.

Carnigan swore gently to himself, hefted the rifle in

his hands and plodded grimly on along the trail. He was careful to keep to the side of the canyon, where the ground was stony, rather than walk in the dust of the trail itself, for he was still uneasy about his back. The Indian who had been left behind – assuming there was only one – might recover and follow. In broad daylight, he would have no trouble picking up Carnigan's tracks. But in moonlight, he might miss them.

That was also assuming that only one Indian had been left behind.

The back of Carnigan's neck did its best to calm down. But the thought of that Ute refused to allow it.

They were savage people, Carnigan thought, as the silver and black slash of the canyon unrolled before him. Mountain dwellers with at least some of the attributes of the Plains Indians.

Like every Indian he had ever encountered, they valued horses to the point of obsession. A Ute man with fewer than half a dozen ponies was counted a poor fellow, and herds of two or three dozen were not unknown.

But they were handsome people, unlike the Navajo and the Apache, who ran to bandy, small men with flat, cruel faces and tubby women. Not always true, he told himself. His Apache wife would have been welcomed and admired at any court in Europe. There was a pang of pain as he remembered her death.

The walls of the canyon were falling away, now, and ahead of him he could see the great silver sea which was the meadow.

17

Soon he stood in the patch of shadow at the mouth of the canyon and looked out across the grass. The night was still and the contrast between the rocky cleft up which he had just walked and the apparent lushness of the meadow was startling.

Beyond, the black bulk of the hills rose up in a fantastic landscape of light slashed with shadow, and, far beyond, the mountains soared.

A man could stand in the fire and look up to the snows, within sight and yet far from his reach. Die of thirst in the sight of enough water to float a sailing-ship.

What a country! Carnigan told himself in awe. What a place!

But the thought of water brought back the nagging misery of thirst again. His mouth was so dry that the mucus was hardening over the back of his palate. His lips felt sore and cracked.

Some miles ahead, against the foothills, there was a spring and a small pool where the trees leaned over the water. The pool seemed to have no outlet, but the acres of grass were more moist there, and the water must be making its way underground to find some water table below the soil, where it was collecting and irrigating the meadow.

There was a tank, too, at Antelope Rock, over to his right, to the West. The Indians would know of both, and might stake out either. Since there were only three of them to the best of his knowledge, it was unlikely that they would watch both. But they might.

The spring was the more attractive proposition. It would be well known to travellers in this part of the Uncompahgres, and the Indians would probably assume that their pickings would be better there.

Unfortunately, it was also the one in a direct line with where he wanted to go. The tank was slightly further away, in the wrong direction, and there was always the chance that it could have been drained since the last rains.

The moon was waning, now, and he felt desperately tired. But he knew he must cover as much ground as he could during the dark hours.

Up here the sun would be just as hot, and when it rose he would start sweating again.

It would have to be the tank, he decided. The chance of Ute watchers there was smaller. And by the time he got to it, he would be in no state to take on three rested, well-fed, well-watered warriors.

On the other hand, he told himself, there was little chance of having to fight anybody at all.

It was midday before he found out he had guessed wrong.

TWO

Carnigan lay in the grass a few hundred yards from the tank at Antelope Rock, and swore bitterly but silently.

Ahead of him, maybe half-way between himself and the water, the grass had been disturbed slightly. The smooth run of the grass-heads was interrupted for maybe a foot or so. It was a tiny detail, but it meant only one thing: somebody was sitting in the grass.

There were two other similar pockmarks in the surface of the meadow. Two plus one made three, and three made Utes. He wondered where their horses were.

Carnigan had approached the tank with elaborate caution. He was so close that he could almost smell the water when he saw the tell-tale patches in the meadow surface.

The Indians had carefully concealed their trail through the grass stems to their places of conceal-ment. But they could do nothing about the nest in which they actually sat.

Carnigan had concealed his own approach by circling and coming in from behind the Rock itself. A loaf of rock, rearing from the soil close to the beginning of the foothills.

Now, he lay by its base and ran a dry tongue over cracked lips, licking longingly at life lying in a blue pool only yards away.

He could withdraw from the rock and go on his way with little chance of the Indians seeing him. But he knew he could not make it to the spring.

On the other hand, with the Indians patiently sitting in the grass, he could not get to the water without being seen. Unless, of course, something distracted the Utes.

He chewed on a grass stem, tantalized by its relative moistness. Like a goddamn horse, he told himself and wondered absently once again where the Indian ponies were. They were horses, not mountain goats. There was no way the Indians could have got their animals up to the top of the rock.

He searched around him, angry now with himself for not being able to solve a relatively simple problem.

The rock was like a cathedral, standing there in the sea of grass, towering over the pool. Its crest was riven and blasted by weather. There were clefts and crevices in its sides where a man might hide, but a horse never.

From the top of the pile, he thought, he would be able not only to see for miles but would be able to look down on the Indians in their grass nests.

He gave a painful grin, which hurt his lips. His

mind was working slowly and creakily, the effects, he knew, of dehydration. He examined the idea from all sides.

Climb up the rock on the blind side from the Utes. Survey the area. Find the horses.

He cut a thong from the fringe of the buckskin shirt, made a sling for the Henry, and hung it over his shoulder.

Then he retreated to the back of the rock where a twisting crack in the rock surface made a promising ladder, and started to climb.

In good health he would have completed the climb within a couple of minutes. In his weakened state it took him nearly ten, and when, panting, he reached for the top of the crack, he froze in mid-motion.

Strong as a polecat, there came to him the unmistakable smell of Indian.

Instantly , he knew exactly where the Indians' ponies were. And the Indians probably knew where he was.

He clung to the face of the rock, sweating. Ironic that his salivary glands should have produced no saliva, but his sweat glands could bucket out moisture like this.

Very low, almost on the fringe of hearing, a bird called from close by. Except that no bird would be landing on the top of Antelope Rock while the three Indians were there.

The call was repeated three times and then, from directly above his head, answered.

The Indians were 'talking' to one another. So they

must have detected him. But if that were so, why not have killed him before?

The bird-call came again, from overhead, and suddenly Carnigan lost his temper.

He had been pursued by outlaws, ambushed by Indians, lost his outfit, walked twenty miles, been too hot, too cold and too thirsty, and had a practical joke played on him by Indians.

'Enough is enough, by damn!' he roared, and sprang up the last pitch of the rock, drawing his handgun as he went.

He bounded over the lip of the rock, gun in hand, to find a startled Indian right in front of him – facing away from him.

No time to wonder. Carnigan fired into the man, fired again as the prone body gave a great muscular spasm, and turned to snap a shot at another figure which was rising from the rock a few feet away.

He heard a gun roar, felt the burn of a crease along his side, and fired a fourth time, knocking the target sideways. The Ute staggered, levering his rifle with a jerky movement. Carnigan stepped sideways over the dead Indian at his feet, and shot a fifth time. The Ute dropped like a sack.

Another bullet from the third man went past Carnigan's head as he moved, throwing himself flat on the rock, clawing at the thong to get his own rifle into action, knowing he was too late. He saw the third Indian rise, the rifle stock cuddled to his cheek to fire down at Carnigan. Then the Ute's head disintegrated, and the suddenly nerveless body toppled over side-ways over the side of the rock and vanished.

In the ensuing silence Carnigan clearly heard the dropped rifle clatter on the rock, and the thump as the Indian hit the ground on the far side of the rock.

Stunned, he lay where he was for a moment, then reloaded the pistol and pulled his rifle from his shoulder before making his way to the rim and peering cautiously down.

Below, close to the edge of the pool, a party of men and horses was caught in frozen positions.

Carnigan stared at them. All heads were raised and faces turned towards the rock. As he moved, a rifle snapped, and a bullet squealed from the rock near his head.

'Hold your fire!' he roared. 'Don't shoot!' He waved his hat angrily, and the party below, after a moment, waved back.

'C'mon down!' The bellow from below was surprise mixed with anger. Carnigan waved his hat a second time, and stood up, warily. In the fringed shirt, from down there he would be mistaken for an Indian, and someone down there was not only a fine shot, but damned trigger-happy, too.

He turned away from the rim and went to the Indians. The man he had shot first was dead, had been dead from the first shot. Carnigan's second had been unnecessary, and had left him with an empty revolver when the third man could have killed him. He shook his head angrily at his own recklessness, and stepped over to examine the second man. He, too, was dead.

The newcomers were waiting for him at the bottom of the cleft as he slid down, a group of hard-looking men in dirty jeans and checked shirts. But their canteens were wet, he saw. Water was what they had come for, and water was what they had got.

'What happened?' The leader was a tall man, almost as tall as Carnigan himself, though with bony, narrow shoulders and a curious, high-hunched posture. He wore two guns, tied down and the retaining thong had been pulled over the hammer spur.

'Ambush,' Carnigan told him flatly. He reached for the man's canteen. 'Gi' me a drink, for the love o' God.'

The man unhooked the canteen and handed it over, watching while Carnigan lifted it, sipped and rolled the water round his mouth.

'How long ya bin without?'

'Couple o' days.' Carnigan drank again, sparingly.

'Take it easy, then. Don't want to make yo'self sick.' The man grinned. 'I seen a man kill hisself drinking too much after a drought, once.'

He was right. Instinct told Carnigan to upend the canteen and pour the liquid down his throat to his parched body. Reason told him he must not.

'How you come to be here?' It was the small man, thin and sinewy, with a snaggle tooth to the side of his mouth, and several days' growth of beard straggling down into the neck of his shirt.

In the wild a man sometimes had to go without a

shave or a wash for days on end, but these men smelled nearly as strong as the Indians.

Carnigan's drinking gave him time to look around the band and what he saw was nothing but trouble.

Besides the tall leader and the little man, there was a thickset bearded man with a broken hat. He was watching Carnigan expressionlessly, and Carnigan made a mental note of his position.

Beyond the group, holding the horses, was a fourth figure. He was a Mexican or a Spaniard, with a big, floppy sombrero and the short-cut, elaborate coat favoured by Californios

'I said—'

'I heard you.' He raised the canteen again, and drank sparingly. He could feel his body responding to the liquid like a parched plant.

'Well?'

'Well what?'

The little man was getting impatient.

'How did you come to be here?'

'They shot my horse two days back, other side of the pass. I walked. How d'you come to be here your-selves?'

'You askin' us to believe you got hit by the Utes and then come all the way up to catch 'em?' The man was openly contemptuous.

Carnigan refilled the canteen a third time, and handed it back to the tall man.

'I ain't askin' you to believe nothin', mister,' he said quietly. 'You asked me a question, and I answered it. If you don't like the answer, you shouldn't oughta asked the question.'

The Mexican sniggered. 'You ask for that one, *amigo*,' he said jeeringly, and Carnigan saw the flash of fury in the little man's eyes. This one was deadly, like a scorpion. And yet he made no other reaction to the Mexican's gibe.

'Good thing for you we come along,' said the bearded man in a rumbling bass. 'That was a right pretty shot fixed that Injun for you.'

Carnigan nodded. 'Your shot?'

The bearded man shook his head. 'Natchez,' he rumbled, jerking his thumb at the Mexican.

Carnigan nodded towards the Mexican. 'Thanks, *amigo*. Appreciate the shootin',' he said.

Natchez nodded, expressionless. 'There was more than one shot from up there,' he pointed out. 'More Indians?'

'Two.' Carnigan stood up, careful not to turn his back or put down his rifle. The bearded man was bending over the body of the Indian who had fallen from the rock. As Carnigan approached he straightened up, wiping a knife on the side of his trousers. In his hand was a hank of black hair.

'Two more, you say?' He looked up at the rock. 'Hard climb?'

Carnigan jerked his head. 'Far side o' the rock. There's a cleft you can get a hold of. You scalp hunters?'

The bearded man grinned a sly grin. 'All kinds o'

things. But ha'r's ha'r, and they pays up to two hundred dollars a hank, down towards Alamosa.'

Carnigan shrugged. 'Help yo'self. But don't be catched with 'em on you, if the Utes turn up.'

Like most men, he was disgusted by the practice of scalp hunting, which was encouraged by the Mexican government and by some local administrations even in the States. He had seen whole Indian villages wiped out by the men who collected the grisly trophies and turned them in for the bounty.

Theoretically, the bounty was offered only for the scalps of hostile warriors, but a hank of hair cannot speak to identify itself. A woman's hair or that of a child looked much the same as a full-blooded Apache warrior, and was a great deal less trouble to collect.

The bearded man climbed the rock and returned with his trophies. Carnigan had built and lighted a cigarette, and waited in the shade for developments.

He did not have long to wait.

'Horse dead, huh?' It was the little man again. Carnigan watched him out of the corner of his eye. The Mexican, Natchez, was one step ahead of the rest in his thinking, and his eyes were searching the surrounding grasslands minutely. He was looking for the Indian ponies. It wouldn't be long before he had worked out where they were.

'Adam ain't no deader,' he told the little man.

'You'd have to ride double with one of us, if you want to get out of here.' The tall leader spoke softly. Carnigan noted his turn of phrase.

'No need,' he said flatly. 'I got me a horse, now. I got three.'

The Mexican shot him a look of understanding. The other three men stared at him.

'What . . . you mean, the Indian ponies? Where the hell are they?' asked the bearded man, realizing for the first time that the Utes would not have walked.

'Close by,' Carnigan told him. 'They laid 'em down in the grass while they was waitin'.'

'Waitin' for you?' It was the leader again.

'Not me. That bunch was waitin' for you,' Carnigan said. 'Reason I was able to come up behind 'em was they'd no idea I was around. They was waitin' for you, and they'd a got you, too. You didn't know they was there, and they sure as hell knew you was.'

The Mexican was staring fixedly at one of the pock-marks in the grass which Carnigan had noticed earlier. It was not the hiding place of an Indian, as he had originally thought, but that of a horse.

Carnigan stood up and walked rapidly to the nearest of the nests. As he approached, he could see the horse's flank through the tops of the grass stems, and hear its muffled whickering.

The horse had been laid on its side, and its head and legs secured to three picket pegs driven deep into the ground. Blindfolded, its mouth tied with rawhide, it was helpless, and invisible save from very close up. Keeping his side to the scalp hunters, who had followed him, he cut free its hoofs, stepping back sharply as the horse kicked convulsively, and then cut free its head.

When he had calmed it, he looped the bridle over his arm and moved on to the next.

'I'll be damned. What d'you make o' that, Reno?' The little man was chuckling, watching while Carnigan roused the second pony, and moved on to the third.

The Mexican stood a little apart from the others, and watched carefully while Carnigan roused the third horse, and then knotted the lead reins of the second and third together.

In a moment, Carnigan knew it would occur to the scalphunters that – far from being dismounted – Carnigan was now the owner of three horses.

Two of them were typical Indian ponies, scrubby and strong, but creatures of no great beauty. But the third, the last to be found, was a grulla, a mouse-coloured horse with good lines and powerful haunches.

The horse had obviously been trained to the saddle and he found the marks where a double cinch had been used. There was a brand on its hip, too, a double letter D interlaced.

'Double Dee. That's Red River Darker's brand,' said the bearded man. 'Disappeared last spring, up in the San Juans. I reckon we know what happened to him then.' He spat into the grass.

'Mount up, mister. It's time we was movin'.'

Carnigan hesitated. The last thing he wanted was to join this band. But if he refused they would want to know why.

On the other hand, tagging along with them meant keeping his eyes open. They would kill him with as little compunction as would the Utes. There was his rifle, his pistol and now his horses from which they might profit. And they would assume he was carrying money. To men like these, that was triple reason to kill.

'Where you headin'?' he asked, to cover the moment of indecision.

'Copperhead Tanks and Kellerman's,' said the leader, briefly. 'Best come along with us, mister. If them Utes got mates round here, they won't stop to ask who dropped their pals and took their hair.'

Carnigan swung his leg over the grulla, and hung on while the horse instantly did its best to dump him flat on his back. It was a breathless, jolting three or four minutes, and the scalp hunters watched with awe until the dust-cloud came to a standstill, and Carnigan emerged from it, still riding the horse.

' 'E like you,' said Natchez. 'You still there.'

Carnigan trotted over to the other two ponies, standing ground-hitched, and took the lead rein.

'I'll ride back marker,' he said. 'That way if this bastard cuts loose again, I got room to let 'im run.'

That way, too, he would not have any of those pairs of hard, ruthless eyes looking at his back. It was a point not overlooked by the stoop-shouldered leader. He gave a flicker of a smile.

'Suit yo'self,' he said. 'I'm Reno Styles. That's Mart

31

Donner, and the guy with the snag in his mouth's Brinsley. He's Natchez,' he added, jerking a thumb at the Mexican.

The Mexican grinned, flashing surprisingly good teeth.

'*Encantado, señor. . . ?*'

'Carnigan.'

'Señor Carnigan. Ees good to meet you. You know horses.'

'Yeah.' Carnigan watched while they moved out, riding in line ahead, then joined on the end of the line.

THREE

Copperhead Tanks, up in the Uncompahgres, was a collection of small tarns, spread among the trees, rather than tanks in the true sense of the word. It was there that Con Kellerman had decided that a campaigning life was not for him, and bought his own discharge from the United States Army.

The hard-working miners and trappers who passed by the Tanks, on the other hand, deserved Con's closest attentions, and they flocked to get it.

For Con Kellerman was a cook. A cook of fame and renown, and justly so.

His pies and pastries melted in the mouths of men who had lived for months on beans and bacon fried in a skillet over the flames of a wood fire. His buffalo steaks were famous, and his doughnuts a legend.

Kellerman's trading post, standing between two of the larger tanks, backed by the mountains and looking out over a valley which dropped away for nigh on a thousand feet, was a small fort in itself. Kellerman started with a blockhouse built of stripped logs on a stone foundation, and added one more building at a time.

There were horses in the corral near the barn, and saddles on the top rails.

'Half a dozen, I make it,' Reno said casually, swinging down from the saddle and tossing his reins to Natchez, who caught them and alone of the group made no attempt to get down from his mount.

Donner and Brinsley followed their leader up the steps to the main trading post which doubled as a saloon and where, at long tables, Kellerman's hungry customers took their food.

'You comin', Carnigan?' Reno made it sound casual, but there was that about the posture of the others which warned Carnigan it was not an incidental question.

'Sure.' He pulled the blankets off the Indian ponies, and turned them, along with the grulla, into the corral. Natchez was unsaddling his own mount. The other three remained saddled and bridled at the hitching rail, as though their owners expected a quick departure.

It did not make sense that Natchez was rubbing down his own horse, though, clearly preparatory to spending the night here.

Carnigan kicked his tired brain into action, and walked slowly up the steps to the trading post. He had managed to catnap in the saddle over the last eighteen hours, but had remained awake most of the night, unwilling to trust his companions.

Here at Kellerman's he would be able to sleep, to replenish his lost supplies and to bid goodbye to the four scalp hunters.

They had talked little on the journey, and then in generalities only, unwilling to reveal too much of themselves to one another.

The land was vast, sprawling and empty. There were relatively few men in it, but those men knew one another or knew of one another better than the citizens of the older, crowded societies of the East or of Europe.

Carnigan crossed the floor of the saloon and put his rifle on the bar.

'Hi, Carnie. Long time.' Kellerman put a shot glass and a bottle of whiskey in front of him without being asked, and Carnigan poured himself a measure while the big man drew a schooner of beer from a barrel on the trestles against the back wall.

The scalp hunters were sitting at a table near the door, with a bottle and glasses. Natchez was not yet with them. They had raised their eyes when Carnigan came in, and nodded at him, but none of them said anything.

Carnigan picked up the beer with his left hand and let his eyes run round the room while he drank.

'See you been building again, Con.'

The fat Irishman laughed. 'Had an immigrant train through in the Spring. They paid me in labour, and I got the best of the deal. There was a master builder among 'em, and two masons.'

Kellerman's sprawling fortress had all been built by his customers. Any man who needed supplies but could not afford to pay for them had the alternative of putting in hours or days of labour on one of the incessant building projects the Irishman had in hand.

'Ya eatin'?' Kellerman swabbed the bar again.

'Sure am. What you got?'

'For you, I got lion steak. Been a big varmint livin' high off my cattle, and I never could get the bastard. Then he tried one of my hawgs last Tuesday, and I ketched him in the open, with that ol' Spencer.'

While he ate Carnigan watched his travelling companions, with a growing sense of unease.

They showed every sign of being relaxed and settled. Like the men at the far end of the room, who were sitting chatting companionably over their coffee, now that the business of eating was over.

Yet outside the door their horses stood saddled and bridled. And it was early evening. It did not make sense for them to move on from here tonight, into the woods where they could only be less comfortable and safe.

'Whiskey with your coffee?' Kellerman leaned over him. 'Who are those guys you rode in with, Carnie?'

'Scalp hunters,' Carnigan told him. 'We both run into trouble with the same bunch o' Utes.'

'What happened?'

'The Utes lost. I got three horses in your corral,

Con, and I'm going to need supplies. Take one of them in exchange?'

Kellerman nodded. 'You know my terms, Carn. I pay by the pound. Don't care what kind o' animal you got there.'

In his situation, Carnigan would have done the same. Kellerman had a small herd of horses which he constantly changed. Incoming travellers often needed a new horse, and would take anything they could get. Sometimes, they left lamed animals in part exchange. Sometimes, simply tired ones.

'It's an Injun pony, Con,' he said. 'Paint. Healthy but he sure ain't no beauty. I'm keeping the other two. There's a grulla, used to belong to Red River Darker. Leastwise, that's what those guys reckon.'

'Red vanished last year in the San Juans,' said Kellerman. 'People reckon the Utes got him. Want I should put the word out?'

'Appreciate it.'

Kellerman would mention the horse to passers by. If the unfortunate Darker or one of his relatives – assuming he had any – needed to know about the horse, he would get the news before too long. It would also establish that Carnigan had not stolen the animal.

'What d'you need?' Kellerman was a storekeeper first and a cook second. 'Wong! Wong! Where the hell is that little yeller . . . Ah! Take the coffee pot round that table, Wong, and keep an eye on the bar, I've got work to do, you spawn o' hell!'

Carnigan grinned as a Chinese in blue pyjamas

padded up the room from the kitchens and carried a coffee-pot the size of a railway engine around the table, filling cups. Kellerman and Wong had been together in the army, and were firm friends. Yet the big Irishman talked as though the Chinese was perpetually idle and troublesome.

'One o' these days, that feller's goin' to dice you up with that damn great axe o' his,' he said. Kellerman grinned.

'Wong?' he said loudly. 'I'll chew him up and spit him out come next big snow. I only keep 'im around in case I run outa bacon.'

Wong came and filled the coffee cups at Carnigan's table.

'I poison you if you chew on me, fat man,' he said expressionlessly. 'Me and whole family live on fat Irishman like you! Next snow, it chow mein time!'

Kellerman waved a fist the size of a leg of lamb. Wong ducked and made his way serenely back to the kitchens with the coffee-pot.

Carnigan spent the next half hour wrangling amiably with Kellerman over the price of supplies.

The deal was closed and Carnigan was just selecting a new saddle from Kellerman's racks when he heard the first sounds of the carriage as it came through the gates.

Hooves hammered out in the compound. There was the crunching of wheels and the jingle of harness. A man's voice was shouting hoarsely.

Carnigan put down a second-hand stock-saddle he

had been considering and walked with Kellerman to the door, to see the dust settling in the evening on a carriage which would not have looked out of place on the Champs Elysées in Paris.

Dismounting from their horses outside were a dozen men in trail clothes. One of them, a square, grey-haired man in dark, neat clothes, was opening the door of the carriage and out of it as Carnigan watched came the most beautiful woman he had ever seen in his life.

Beside him he heard Kellerman swallow hard, and he knew his own expression must be nearly as silly as that of the fat man.

She was stunning in every sense of the word. A honey-blonde head, classical sculptured features, a long, slender neck descending into superbly cut travelling-clothes.

For a moment, she stood in the carriage doorway, surveying the gaping faces which had appeared at the windows.

Then with a tiny smile, she said clearly and coolly:

'Thank you Major Blake. Would you be so kind as to make arrangements for the night?'

And with a graceful inclination of the head, she stepped out of the carriage, and swept up to the steps, across the stoop, and between Carnigan and Kellerman into the post.

The grey-haired man came up the steps in her wake, and nodded curtly at Carnigan and Kellerman.

'You, unhitch that team and stable them right away.'

He made to push between the two men, but Carnigan merely turned his back and walked back to his examination of the saddle. Behind him he heard the man clear his throat angrily.

Kellerman said: 'I wouldn't, Major.'

The woman's voice came then. 'Is there a man around here who might like to earn a little money by doing it for us, then? Our escort really is very tired and has its own duties to perform. Is it possible to eat here?'

'Ma'am,' said Kellerman sincerely, 'you can eat better here'n anywhere this side o' Paris. As for the horses, I'll find somebody for you. Boys!'

Carnigan thought he was going to be trampled to death as almost every man in the room stampeded to the woman's side. Up here, just seeing a woman who was not an Indian squaw was enough. To see a woman as beautiful as this one was an event these men would be talking about all winter.

Carnigan noticed that one of the boxes which was brought in by the mounted escort, instead of being stacked with the rest against the wall of the store, was carried through to the back room where the lady had elected to sleep.

Looking up again, Carnigan caught the eyes of Reno Styles, and instantly he knew why the horses had been left saddled and hitched. The outriders' mounts, on the other hand, had been cleaned, dried and made comfortable for the night, and along with the outriders, the men had returned to the store.

Where there had been desultory conversation before, there was now animated chatter. The outriders had gathered around their own table, and set about their food with serious expressions. They were clearly soldiers out of uniform and enjoying the freedom.

Carnigan waited until Kellerman, fussing like a major-domo with royalty under his roof, had served the travellers' meal, along with champagne cooled in the nearest tarn.

When the fat man returned to his table, full of chatter and awe, Carnigan broached the subject of the scalp hunters.

'Watch yourself, Con,' he said quietly with a nod at the table in the corner where Reno had just called for another bottle. 'I think we're goin' to have trouble.'

Kellerman glanced at him sharply, 'What kind o' trouble?'

'Shooting trouble,' said Carnigan. 'I reckon those boys I come in with are fixin' to rob the lady.'

Kellerman nodded slowly. 'Wondered why they hadn't put up their hosses,' he said slowly. 'What d'you reckon?'

'Search me,' Carnigan told him. 'I got to wondering about those same animals. And when the lady come in, Reno knew her right off. Everybody else is starin' at her wonderin' who she is, and what she's doin' here. But not Reno.

'He was starin' at that box the major brung in. Particular the one they took through to her room. Like it was valuable or somethin'.

41

'More important, as if he knowed right off what it is.'

The two men were talking quietly and by mutual understanding, neither of them so much as glanced at the table in the corner. But Kellerman, through long habit, raised his head and took a long look round the room.

'You realize somethin' else?' he said tersely. 'Every man on the place is in here right now, except for that Mex you come in with. Where the hell's he at?'

He started to rise from his seat, and Reno, without warning or excuse, shot him from across the room.

The bullet took the big man high in the shoulder, and knocked him sideways, across Carnigan's lap just as the scout started to draw. Carnigan was knocked sideways in his turn, off his chair and under the table with Kellerman on top of him.

The coach guards started to get up from their food, and Reno fired again, this time shattering the bottle which had been on the table with them. They froze.

From the woman's room, came a wailing scream, and the door banged open. Standing in the entrance was the lady, and at her head was a shotgun held by Natchez. Of Major Blake there was no sign.

'Stand still!' Reno's voice was oddly high-pitched, but it carried across the hubbub in the long room. 'Keep still, or he'll kill her!'

The men in the room got the message, and the place fell quiet. It was shocked into silence for more than one reason.

The speed of the attack caught everybody by surprise, and most of the men who had sat down to eat had discarded their weapons, hanging them against the walls.

And the idea of the woman being used as a hostage had honestly appalled most of them.

With the speed of a practised robber, Reno moved into the silence.

'Natchez! Bring her over here! Quick!'

The Mexican hustled the woman across the room. Her face was white with shock and her hair had come unwound from its tight, complex style, and hung in golden swags about her shoulders. Carnigan, frozen under the table with Kellerman's bulk hampering his right arm, noticed with surprise that the front of her dress was unfastened.

Slowly and without drawing attention to himself, he began to shift the big Irishman to get out his gun. He stopped when a pistol bellowed, and splinters bit into his cheek.

'Keep still, Carnigan, or I'll drop ya!' It was Brinsley, grinning a snag-toothed grin. The man had hardly taken his eyes off Carnigan since they came in.

The silence grew. From where he lay under the table, Carnigan could hear the woman's sobbing breathing and Kellerman's laboured gasps. The Irishman was losing blood steadily but not very fast. He would live, Carnigan decided. No use to get himself shot, when there was nothing he could do about it.

'You and you!' Reno pointed to two of the men at the end of the room. 'Go into the back room and bring the box out.'

'No!' The woman gave a convulsive leap in Natchez' grasp. The Mexican caught her by the hair and pulled her back. From the men in the room came a low growl, and Reno's gun swung again to cover the end of the room.

Mart Donner moved to one side so that the shotgun he was carrying could cover the room. Carnigan watched the men relax slightly. In a crowded room a man might take a chance with a handgun or a rifle. But nobody was going to jump that double-barrelled Greener.

The two men Reno had detailed emerged from the back room, carrying the box.

'Put it down there!' Reno gestured at the space in front of the bar, walked over to it and shot off the lock.

Reno pulled open the lid and grunted with satisfaction.

'You!' He pointed at one of the men. 'Put that in those bags.'

From the box came a succession of small money-bags, and the kneeling man packed them, two at a time, into four sets of saddle-bags which had until now hung from Kellerman's racks.

When he had finished, Reno gestured at the door.

'Load 'em up!'

Obediently, the man took the bags to the door, two at a time. When he reappeared, Reno grinned.

'We'll be on our way now, gents,' he said cheerily. 'I hear anybody follerin' up our trail tonight, and the lady gets ventilated. Don't doubt it – I'll drop her soon as look. You can pick her up at dawn tomorrow over t' Hangman's Ridge a ways. If I don't decide to keep her with us a while. Just in case you don't think I mean what I say, there's this!'

He turned and fired twice into the chest of the man who had carried the bags out to the horses. The man dropped without a sound, and Reno surveyed the stunned faces of the waiting men.

'I mean what I say,' he said. 'Think on it.'

They backed to the door, and the woman gave a despairing cry as she was dragged from the room.

Outside, they could hear the horses' hoofs hammering as the hold-up men rode off through the gate.

For a long moment there was silence, and then pandemonium broke loose. Despite the robbers' warning, men ran for the corral to catch their horses – and discovered their animals had been taken. One man actually started running after the fugitives, but after a few steps realized the pointlessness of his task and came back.

Carnigan shifted Kellerman off himself, and helped one of the guards to sit the big man on a chair and pull off his shirt.

The fat Irishman was the colour of lard, and sweating heavily. Carnigan poured whiskey into the wound.

'Shock,' said Carnigan briefly. 'I seen it before. Get

45

some coffee into him, and tell Wong to bring me some water and a bottle of whiskey.'

He poured some of the whiskey into a cup and soaked a strip of cloth in it, while examining the wound. The bullet had gone in the front at an angle and glanced off a bone, emerging at the top.

'Nasty wound,' he told Kellerman. The fat man nodded.

'Not as nasty as it would a been if I hadn't stood up. He was aimin' for my haid,' he said painfully. 'I shouldn't a looked at 'em. Tipped 'em off.'

Carnigan agreed with him. But the whole affair had moved so slickly that he was certain it had been planned just this way.

'You may have speeded up their plans a mite,' he told Kellerman. 'But they was fixin' for this anyways. Take a hold there.'

Kellerman's face went pasty again as his wound was swabbed out with the raw spirit. A splinter of bone came out of the hole with some dark blood, and Carnigan peered closer.

'Pity it ain't straight, and I could go through it with an arrer,' he said almost to himself and Kellerman shuddered.

'Bind 'er up, Carnie,' he said. 'Wong's a good nurse. He'll keep an eye on me.'

Carnigan tied up the wound, and stood up to look at the circle of faces in the lamplight.

'Where's Major Blake?' he asked. Blank incomprehension stared back at him.

'Blake was in there with the lady,' he said. 'Anybody seen him?'

Blake was on the floor in the back room. He had been hit over the head with something, probably a gun barrel, and there was a hard lump under the broken skin.

Carnigan probed it gently, raised a groan from the wounded man, but found no sign of the sponginess which would have meant a cracked skull.

'You bin lucky,' he commented. 'What happened?'

Blake gazed at him with slow-clearing eyes.

'Somebody hit me,' he said stupidly. 'Who hit me?'

'Natchez, I reckon,' said Carnigan. 'How did he get into the room, Blake?'

'Tapping at the window,' said the soldier. 'Tapping at the window, and I went to see what it was. I can't . . .'

'Remember anything else,' supplied Carnigan. 'But I can guess. You opened the window and looked out. Couldn't see nothin', so you stuck your head out to see further.'

'Yes, that's right. And then . . . Marion! Where's Miss Crawshaw?'

'Then the lights went out,' Carnigan finished. 'And now, so has Miss Crawshaw. That'd be General Crawshaw's daughter, I'd guess?'

'It would. Where is she?'

'By this time, she's half-way to someplace else in bad company,' Carnigan told him and finished off wiping the man's head.

'Put a bandage round that so he can wear his hat,

47

Wong,' he said tiredly. He straightened up and eased his back.

'Are my men after them?' Blake was trying to see round the room. 'How far can they have got?'

'They took her and the money from your strong-box, and they said they was going towards Hangman's Ridge,' Kellerman told him. The soldier started to pull himself to his feet and staggered wildly, falling back on to the chair.

'And nobody is after them? Are you mad? Marion . . . and . . . and the payroll, too! The general will go berserk! Carnigan! Carnigan! Get after them, man! O'Hara! Saddle up!'

'Sit down, O'Hara,' Carnigan said as one of the escort started for the door. 'What the hell you plannin' to saddle up, anyways? Some of the hawgs? Them horses is scattered all to hell and gone, when they rode off. And say you catch a couple in the dark in the woods, how you goin' to foller them men? You can't see to track, and you don't know the ground.

'And if you did catch up with 'em, override 'em in the dark mebbe. You think they wouldn't kill Miss Crawshaw? They'd kill her soon as look, and you too.'

'They'd kill a woman?' Blake was incredulous.

'That bunch are scalp hunters. They've killed women folks by the score. Children, too. When that kind go through a village, they don't leave nothin' to tell the tale, not even the dawgs.'

'Indian women, squaws, maybe. But Miss Craw-shaw—'

'Is a right nice bit of woman-flesh, and they ain't goin' to kill her yet. Not while they're plannin a bit o' fun to go with their cash. Tonight, they'll move as far and as fast as they can. Then they'll hole up for the day, watch their back trail.

'They see someone comin', they'll kill the girl, and split up. Leave several trails to follow and arrange to meet up later. Maybe twenty miles away, maybe a hundred and twenty. You'll lose 'em.'

Blake had pulled himself together with amazing speed. He was a tough, strong man and he had lost two precious things. Now he needed to get them back.

'O'Hara. Go outside and see if this man is right, and the horses really have gone. Kowalski and Glitton, you'll ride scout. Craig—'

'Craig's dead, Major. And we seen the horses was run off when we went out after the fugitives,' O'Hara told him. 'They're scattered out in the dark. Carnigan's right, sir, we wouldn't find one in the dark, and some of them at least will likely come back at daylight. Give us a chance to catch the rest, and get after 'em properly.'

Blake walked over to look down at Craig. Somebody had thrown a blanket over him, and Wong was spreading sawdust to soak up the blood.

'How did he get killed? Resisting the bastards?'

'Never raised so much as his voice agin' 'em,' Carnigan told him. 'Kinda strange, that. But I reckon he musta bin the one as tipped 'em off about you.'

49

Blake glared at him. 'Tipped 'em off? What d' you mean by that?'

Carnigan sat down and began to roll himself a cigarette.

'Well, now, Major, this here's the way I see it. I ran into that bunch of outlaws yesterday, up to Antelope Rock. We were havin' a dust up with a party of Utes, and sort o' come together that way.

'They was headed here, so I tagged along with them. Never know how many Utes are out, and there's safety in numbers. Anyways, there wasn't no way of breakin' off from them without showin' them my back, and I didn't get to my ripe old age by turning my back on men like that.

'Now, when we got here to Kellerman's, I stripped down my horses and put 'em in the corral, and so did Natchez. The others put theirs at the hitchin' rail, and left 'em with their saddles on.'

He twisted the paper and put the end of the cigarette into his mouth, lighting it with a match struck on the underside of the table.

'I thought at the time it was in case they come across somebody in here that they knowed. Men like that are mostly on the run from someone, somewheres. They need to take off kinda sudden, time to time. Real cautious, they are.

'Natchez, he was the look-out and the wrangler. They was fixin' to ambush you right here, tonight, and they done just that.'

'But you said yourself that Natchez stripped the

saddle off his own horse and turned it into the corral.'

'He sure did. But then, that horse of his was limpin' a bit all day. And they was some nice horses in that corral. Including a grulla I only got myself yesterday. I reckon Natchez just waited until you was all in here eatin' and helped hisself to another horse. A fresh one without a limp. And another for Miss Crawshaw.

'Then he walked round to the back room, which is the logical one to put a woman guest in, and tapped on the window and out come your head, Major, just askin' to be rapped on with somethin' about the shape of a rifle butt.'

Blake sat and stared at him for a long time. Then he gave an injudicious shake of his head. For a moment, his eyes fogged with pain.

'Impossible. How could they have known that we were coming? I kept the route entirely to myself and the—'

'And the sergeant and the coach driver. I'd put money Craig was drivin' that there fancy rig out there.'

Blake nodded, sickly.

'He was. And he was very keen we should be right on schedule, all along the route.'

'Sure he was. He was keepin' an appointment with a hell of a lot o' money. I expect they promised him a share in that at least. And he would be in the way when it come to sharin' out the girl.'

Blake began to get to his feet again, his mouth working.

'Sit down, Major. Nothin' ain't goin' to happen to that lady tonight. Probably not even tomorrow. At the moment all them scalp hunters is thinkin' about is gettin' clean away.'

'But they mentioned Hangman's Ridge. At least you must know where that is?'

'Sure I do, but I'm just as sure that they ain't goin' nowhere near Hangman's. That was just to make sure if anybody did catch a horse tonight and got goin' he'd be safely goin' in the wrong direction.'

Blake was beside himself. At the very moment, thought Carnigan, he would start wringing his hands in despair.

'But what are we going to do?' he said.

Carnigan stretched his six-foot length and reached for the blankets he had traded out of Kellerman only a few hours before.

'Speakin' personal, Major, I'm goin' to get me a few good hours sleep. Come dawn, when we know how we're fixed for horses and can see, I'll track them outlaws down for you myself if you want. Until then, I'm restin' all I can. I'd advise you to do the same.'

FOUR

'Hold up!' Carnigan raised his hand and the line of mounted men behind him pulled to a standstill. He slipped from the saddle and crouched by the trail, turning over twigs and leaves and casting in ever-widening circles along the pathway.

It had been a long, hard ride since they tracked down their scattered horses. But at least he was fairly certain they were close to the point where the men they were following had stopped for their first camp.

'They sure made good time,' he told Sergeant O'Hara, who was riding point with him. The big soldier grunted and spat a jet of tobacco juice with murderous accuracy at a nearby clump of sumac.

Tracking was a long, slow business. The men he was following were woods-wise and had pulled every trick they knew to lay a false trail. Only Carnigan's superior knowledge of the ground had enabled him to make occasional leaps in logic and catch up.

Twice the men ahead had struck off at right angles

to their own line of march. Once, they had doubled back upon themselves. Once, they had split up, leaving two diverging sets of tracks.

'And all that was in the dark, when they couldn't be sure they'd covered up real good,' Carnigan mused. 'These guys are clever.'

'Never mind giving the bastards medals. Just catch 'em and I guarantee you they'll stop being clever real quick,' said O'Hara, flatly.

Both the sergeant and his little detachment of soldiers in civilian clothes were taking the abduction of Marion Crawshaw as a deeply personal insult.

'What made Blake bring a woman like that up here?' Carnigan asked O'Hara as he and the sergeant climbed back into the saddle and gestured the impatiently waiting line forwards.

'She's General Crawshaw's daughter,' said O'Hara. 'The Major is an ambitious man. He reckons the promotion he wants could come easier if he makes up to the right woman.'

He broke off as the two men urged their horses up a steep, narrow defile. They had pulled a good deal ahead of the main body again and when they topped out they pulled up to let their horses breathe.

'Major Walls, he wanted to send the money with a full escort as usual. But Major Blake, he reckoned he could get it through safer by movin' faster. Fewer men, a fast-movin' carriage and route only he knew before we set out.'

Carnigan finished building a cigarette, twisted the

end with a practised twirl of the fingers, and lit the smoke holding the match inside his cupped hands.

'So he told you and Craig where he was goin' to be and when,' he said.

O'Hara's face clouded.

'Yeah. I wondered about Craig at the time. Said he needed to know to fix the carriage for the trip.'

'And he passed on the news to the boys,' added Carnigan. 'They musta thought it was Christmas, knowin' the girl was comin' along an' all.'

O'Hara looked sick. 'She only decided to come at the last minute,' he said. 'We was takin' the carriage through to the General at San Luis anyways.'

He followed Carnigan up the trail for a while in silence.

'You reckon she'll be all right?' he asked in the end. 'I known that girl since she was so high. She's sassy but she's kinda cute, you know?'

Carnigan let the grulla pick its own way while he searched the sides of the path for signs that the fugitives had turned aside yet again. Up ahead, the mountain bulked, tree-covered and massive, and above the tree line, he could see the true obstacles ahead of them.

'We ain't seen their camp yet,' he pointed out. 'So they been pushin' theirselves as hard as they can. They expect to be followed. They won't have time for fun and games, yet. If we keep pushing as hard as we can, we can keep them on the move and they won't be able to stop and . . . and do anything to her.'

The knowledge that revenge was following fast might distract a man's mind admirably.

He hoped.

'You sure?'

'Sure I'm sure,' he said, irritably. 'Why do you think I'm layin' on the pace? For fun?'

The devil of it was that he was not so sure. But then, it was not Carnigan who had brought a beautiful woman and a chest of treasure into the Uncompahgres with an escort of only a dozen or so men and a carriage which must have been the wonder of every Indian and passing prospector for miles.

'A virgin and a bag o' gold,' he muttered to himself. 'I reckon a man like Reno could smell that combination through a range o' mountains a hundred miles upwind in a snowstorm.'

All they needed then was a couple of bottles, and the scalp hunters had taken at least two from Kellerman's when they left.

He pulled up the horses and dismounted again. He hunkered down to examine first the ground and then the terrain ahead. O'Hara prudently reined in his horse so that it could not overrun the trail of the men ahead, and waited.

'They camped over there,' Carnigan said, standing to ease his back. 'We'll go and take a look round, then wait for the major to catch up.'

When Blake and the remaining men rode into the little clearing among the pines, it was to find a small fire burning and a pot of coffee on the side. He reined in and let the men line up by his side.

'Just what in hell do you think you're doing, Carnigan?' he asked, his voice barely controlled.

The scout looked up at him from under the brim of his hat, and let a plume of smoke trickle out from his nostrils before he answered.

'Why, I'm letting my horse rest a mite, Major,' he said mildly. 'And while he's doin' that, I'm takin' a break my own self and enjoyin' a cup of coffee. There ain't goin' to be rest or coffee where we're goin' and within the next hour or so you and the men are goin' to need both.'

Blake dropped from his horse, the suppressed rage making his movements jerky, but otherwise under control.

He strode to the fire and raised his foot to kick the coffee-pot across the clearing, spraying hot coffee as it went. Carnigan watched it go with regret.

'Damn you! Damn you, Carnigan!' Blake blazed. 'Those men up there are holding a woman. A beautiful woman. She must not remain in their hands a moment longer than she has to. And you sit here drinking coffee and taking your ease?'

Carnigan rose with a liquid grace and walked across the clearing to retrieve the pot. He brought it back, stood it in the coals with a gloved hand, and reached for his canteen.

'Reno and the boys,' he said as he refilled the pot, 'camped here last night, late. They made some coffee, ate jerky and they watched their back trail a while.

Three of them had a smoke. One was on guard.

'Natchez – the guy who turned your lights out – eased the horses and took them over to the spring over there for a drink. The flow's constant, but it ain't strong, so he took them two at a time, which took him a long time.

'Miss Crawshaw sat down over here and had coffee as well. She was talkin' to one of them. Reno, I'd guess, but I ain't sure because I ain't sorted their tracks too exact, yet. But I'm gettin' to know them.

'They was here about a couple of hours and they took it in turns to sleep for a while. Nothin' happened to Miss Crawshaw except she slept. The ground ain't disturbed where she lay, so I'd say she was about exhausted. Ain't surprisin', considering.'

He stirred the fire round the pot.

'Then only about three hours ago, they saddled up, had more coffee and pulled out. They's only one way they can go from here, assuming they didn't double back, and their horses hadn't developed wings.'

He pointed, and the major, seething, was forced to follow his pointing arm. Behind them bulked the mountain barrier, white and beautiful.

'It's cold up here, Major, but it's goin' to get colder up there. The air's thin, and we're high now, but we're goin' a helluva sight higher. The horses can't breathe too good when the air's thin, and neither can you.

'But you ain't carryin' around fifteen stone of dumb cavalryman and all his weapons and kit, so it'll affect the horses a lot worse than you. You push these horses now and you'll catch up with Reno all right. You'll crawl up to him on your hand and knees.'

He swilled the pot around in his hand, and poured coffee into his cup.

'One thing that'll keep you goin' this far up is coffee. Keep your heart goin' and it keeps you awake when all you want to do is lie down in the snow.

'When are you goin' to get the message, Major? That ain't no bunglin' fool on the run up there. That Reno, he planned all this weeks ago, before you even got started on your damn-fool scheme to come up into some of the most rugged country on earth with a box full of money and the girl.

'He suborned a member of your force, Major. He picked the weakest one, but the one who would have to know where you was goin' and when you was goin' to get there. He outguessed you, he outmanoeuvred you, and now he's plannin' on outrunnin' you. You are so all-fired eager to co-operate with his plans, I declare, Major, it makes a body wonder how you come to make Major atall.'

Outraged, Blake started forward, ignoring O'Hara's muffled murmur of warning. But Carnigan raised his head and stared at him. Blake had seen eyes like that before in his life, when he visited a zoo back East and looked at some wolves. As he stared, the big male had raised his head and stared back with eyes so pitiless that even with bars between them, Blake had stepped back a pace.

'You put your boot to me or anythin' of mine ever

59

again, Major, and I swear the US Cavalry is goin' to
come up one major short. I ain't funnin', Major.'

He turned his back, and stepped with a rangy stride
to where his horse cropped grass. From the saddle-
bags he took coffee and added a handful to the water
in the coffee pot. One by one, the men helped themselves to a cup.

Blake stared, humiliated, at Carnigan's uncaring
back. Then he turned abruptly, walked to the edge of
the clearing and swept the slope above them with his
binoculars. He was interrupted after a while by
O'Hara, who handed him a cup of coffee. It was
strong, and surprisingly good, considering the cavalier
way it had been made.

'It seems my education was sadly lacking, Sergeant,'
he said, in an attempt to regain his self-esteem. 'How
could Carnigan possibly be so sure about what
happened here?'

O'Hara took him seriously.

'Matter o' experience, I guess, Major,' he said. He
led the officer back to where the party had entered
the clearing.

'Carnigan and I come into the clearing ridin' wide
of Reno's trail, so's not to mess it up. You followed us,
so you didn't mess it up, either. Looky here, now.'

He pointed to the carpet of needles. They had
largely absorbed the prints of the horses' hoofs, but
here and there they had been scuffed and thrown
aside by the passing riders.

'If you look to one side of the trail, you can see one

horse was walking alongside another. All the rest was in a single line. That there's the led horse. The one Miss Crawshaw's ridin'. She's on a short rein and the weight of her horse and herself is less than the others, so he don't dig in so deep. They make less of an imprint, see?'

Blake nodded, irritably. He was not a fool, though at the moment he felt foolish, but if there was something to be learned, he admitted if only to himself that he should devote himself to learning it.

'I see that, but what about the rest of the things? The man on guard is just common sense, I suppose. He could have guessed that.'

O'Hara shook his head.

'Ain't no guesswork about Carnigan,' he said. 'He reads this country like you read a book. That guard, now, he had a broken boot heel. We seen his sign before when he stopped off to look at the back trail a few times and waited.

'He's a short man, so he takes short strides. Measure yours and look how much longer it is than his. Favours his right foot, too. Carnigan says his name's Brinsley and he's dangerous. He waited just here.'

He pulled back a low hanging branch and in the exposed ground beneath it Blake could see the imprint of the boots. One heel had a jagged mark across it, and there were several cigarette butts.

'Miss Crawshaw waited over here.' O'Hara led the now fascinated Major across the clearing to a rock which poked its domed head through the carpet of needles. By the rock were two cigarette butts, both of them stained with saliva.

'Miss Crawshaw don't smoke, and if she did she wouldn't spit on the ends,' said O'Hara. 'So she was talkin' to somebody else. Ain't likely Reno would leave her alone with Natchez or Donner. So Reno spits on his smokes. We'll know him again.'

He straightened up and pointed across the clearing. 'They's a half-chewed end of jerky over there, and there was coffee-grounds in the fire when we found it, so they was eatin' jerky and drinkin' coffee.'

He wiped his hands on the seat of his trousers.

'Ain't no magic to it, Major. No guesswork, neither. The trick is learnin' what to look for and knowing what it is when you see it.'

Blake was intelligent enough to know he had just learned a valuable lesson. It did not damp down his irritation with Carnigan, though.

'Who exactly is Carnigan, O'Hara? You sound as if you know him.'

O'Hara took off his hat and wiped the inside of the band with his bandanna. He put the hat back on again, settled it fore and aft, and gave the officer a level look.

'Carnigan never told his story to anybody, Major,' he said. 'But out here, it's a small community. There ain't that many people around, and you get to know, or know of, pretty well all of them.

'Carnigan is a known man. He scouted for the

Cavalry in the last campaign down South in the Dragoons and the Chiricahuas with Crook when he took out after the Apaches. They say he lived with the Injuns for a while. Had an Injun wife, even. Well, maybe. He knows more about Injuns than any man I ever met, that's for certain.

'He was sheriff of Hammerhead for a while, and that was one hard, fast town. The Anderson bunch was riding down there, back then. They ain't now. He shot two, hanged three and cleaned up the town.

'I heard tell he is a travelled man, too. Bin in Europe, India, down in Mexico, fightin'. Speaks Spanish like a native, Apache, too. One thing, Major. He sure ain't a man to cross. When he said not to take your boot to him again, he weren't funnin'. No way.

'Sorry, Major. But that's the way it is.'

Blake admitted to himself that he had come close to committing a literally fatal error.

But he had already been more intimate with a non-commissioned officer than he normally allowed himself. Instinct made him withdraw the brief contact.

'Thank you O'Hara,' he said formally. 'Now, if the horses are rested enough, we'll move out. Make sure the canteens are filled and every man has warm clothing ready. As Carnigan says, it's going to be cold up there.'

O'Hara joined Carnigan as the party made ready to mount up. The two men surveyed one another silently for a moment, and then by mutual consent they led off into the pines again, drawing immediately ahead of the party.

'Major was curious about you,' O'Hara told the scout as their horses dropped into single file. Carnigan gave him a lopsided grin.

'Seems typical of the man that he didn't ask his damned questions until the day after he shoulda done,' he commented.

They rode in silence for a while and then O'Hara spoke again.

'Don't be too hard on him, Carnie,' he said quietly. 'He ain't a Westerner, and he's worried hisself hairless over Miss Crawshaw and the money. If he don't come back with the cash he'll get broke, and if anything's happened to the girl, he'll wish he had been.

'The general'll pin his hide to the cookhouse door. That feller's got hisself between a rock and a hard place.'

Carnigan grunted. 'He kicks my coffee pot again, he's gonna think that general's Santy-Clause!' he threw over his shoulder. 'Hold up, I ain't too sure about this!'

He stepped out of the saddle and squatted down in the trail. O'Hara waited patiently while the scout turned over twigs and pine needles in a seemingly random pattern.

Carnigan gave an almost soundless whistle.

'I got a feelin' we done picked ourselves up some Injuns,' he said. 'If I'm right, they're betwixt us and Reno. Step carefully, O'Hara.'

They walked their horses on up the trail. O'Hara noticed how Carnigan kept shifting in his saddle and scanning the trees they had passed as well as those they were approaching.

'What d'ye think now?' he asked, stopping to cut himself a plug of chewing tobacco.

'I think we got more company,' said Carnigan. 'And I ain't sure they're Utes.'

O'Hara began to develop a sympathetic unease himself. When Carnigan stopped to examine the trail, he watched carefully for movement instead of just watching the scout.

Carnigan swung into the saddle again. He pulled the Henry from its boot and laid it across his saddle horn, right hand on the action, reins in his left. The horse stepped daintily along the trail, ears pricked and Carnigan watched those ears carefully.

Horses have better hearing than human beings, and this one was listening to something ahead and out of sight, or at any rate listening for something.

His eyes followed a jay, bright with colour, as it swept in from above, and prepared to settle on a low branch in a tree.

At the last moment, the bird flapped frantically and swung away from its intended perch. Carnigan's eyes sharpened.

'Keep goin' O'Hara. They're up ahead, 'bout five hundred yards and off to the right,' he said quietly.

O'Hara paused in the even rhythm of his chewing, and spat off to one side.

'What's the plan?' he said, looking casually from side to side, as he had been periodically for the last few miles. But his hand was covering the breech of his rifle and one finger was within the trigger guard.

'Keep goin' like this until I yell. Then run like hell straight through 'em. The noise'll warn Blake, and he'll take 'em from behind. I hope,' added Carnigan.

'Won't the shootin' warn Reno?'

'Reno knows,' Carnigan said. 'How come nobody wants to take that man seriously? He's been watching us come since we left his last camp site.'

O'Hara gave him an irritated look.

'Damn it, Carnigan,' he said. 'How come you got to spring things like that at times like—'

'GO!' roared Carnigan, and the grulla went off like a cougar after a rabbit, with O'Hara running a length behind and to one side.

At the side of the trail an Indian stood up, drawing a bow. O'Hara fired into him, and saw him drop as he went past.

Carnigan was sitting bolt upright in the saddle, firing the Henry pistol fashion with one hand. He picked off the Indian in the tree who had been betrayed by the jay, swung his horse to one side, guiding him with his knees, and fired again at a running figure cutting in towards the horse's head.

The hillside above was dotted with large boulders, and Carnigan swung the grulla behind one and stopped, sliding immediately from the saddle, and using it as a step to gain the top of the rock.

He dropped to his stomach and fired once, twice over O'Hara's head as the soldier in his turn swerved behind the rock.

Silence fell.

'How many do you reckon?' said O'Hara breathily from the side of the rock.

'I dropped one and you overran another. You get any?'

'One for certain. Another sure ain't as happy this afternoon as he was this mornin'. Many left?'

Carnigan rolled on his back and made a cigarette. As long as he stayed supine, he could not be seen from the fringe of the trees below.

'I made it eight. But they may have been a couple I didn't see,' he said conversationally. He lit the cigarette, took two long, luxurious pulls on it, and rolled back on his chest, putting the lighted cigarette carefully on the rock.

'One thing,' he said, aiming carefully.

'What?'

Carnigan squeezed off a careful shot, and grinned to himself when a brown body fell from the top branches of a tree.

'I was right. They sure ain't Utes.'

From the trees several running figures started up the slope towards them, brown flickers of movement against the darker background, gone as soon as they appeared – but now several yards closer.

Carnigan held his fire, covering the spot where one had vanished.

'What then?' O'Hara had fired and missed and was replacing the used rounds in his carbine.

'Chiricahua Apache, I reckon. A bit far north, but Crook's been stirring 'em up a bit down towards New Mexico.'

'Not Comanche?'

'Not this lot. Apache, and this far west, they should-n't be Jicarillos. Except for . . .'

Another dash by the Indians. Carnigan grunted with annoyance when the man he was waiting for popped up several yards to the right of where he had disappeared.

'Musta rolled over while I was chatterin',' he said bitterly. 'Serves me right.'

There was silence for a while, and then the Apaches popped up again, This time Carnigan had guessed right: his target stopped in mid-stride, and slowly crumpled to the ground.

The rest vanished again. But they were several yards closer.

'You was right about somethin' else, too,' O'Hara told him. Carnigan heard a jet of tobacco juice hit a rock.

'What's that?'

'They was one or two you didn't spot. That one for instance.' O'Hara fired, missed and swore bitterly. The Apaches were closer now.

'Where the hell's Blake?' Carnigan asked tensely. 'We shoulda heard him by now. He can't have been that far behind.'

With a whoop two Apaches over to his right started to run. Carnigan, firing from his right shoulder, had to shift his position and fire awkwardly. Both his shots

68

missed the Indians and they disappeared with derisive yells.

'We're going to have to move,' Carnigan told O'Hara, who was on the left hand side of the boulder and had not seen the Apaches outflank them. 'They's a couple working up behind us.'

O'Hara scrambled round the boulder and surveyed the Indians' new position.

'No way we can pull back a mite out of their line o' fire,' he agreed. 'We'll have to run uphill to the next line of rocks.'

'We could use the horses for cover,' said O'Hara dubiously. Carnigan shook his head, remembered the soldier could not see him, and voiced his objections.

'They'd just shoot the horses and leave us afoot and in the same trouble,' he said.

'I thought Apaches were fond of horses?'

'They are,' said Carnigan. 'But they're fond of ownin' them, and eatin' them, not fond of horses. An Apache in a hurry will be willing to ride a horse to death, eat him, and steal another. He sure ain't goin' to hold his fire just to spare a horse that don't belong to him yet anyway. And those guys will eat any horse they have to shoot. So they'll get the animals anyway.'

He fired carefully into a bush which was very gently changing its position and grinned with satisfaction when it gave a convulsive leap and fell over. There was a spatter of fire from the Indians, but none of them could see him, and none of the shots bothered either of the men.

'You see anythin' of the boys out to the right?' Carnigan asked. O'Hara checked carefully. There was no sign of the two Apaches who had gone uphill.

'Time to worry about Injuns is when you cain't see 'em,' commented Carnigan. 'You keep your eye out for them. They's worse trouble than the ones down here. I'll tell you if anythin' happens downhill.'

There was a lull in the little battle. Carnigan assumed the Indians were counting their dead and treating their wounded after their own fashion. Indian medicine was often brutal but usually effective, and the Indians, who lived in better harmony with their environment than the white men, had an encyclopaedic knowledge of herbs and shrubs.

It suited his purpose, anyway. The longer he and the big sergeant could hold off the Apaches, the more chance there was of Blake catching up and turning the tables.

He wondered for the umpteenth time where on earth the ambitious major was. The group could only have been a little way behind them. It was possible, of course, that Carnigan himself had been caught between two groups of Indians, and that Blake had been ambushed by another group.

'You hear anythin', O'Hara?' he said quietly.

O'Hara grunted a negative. 'Nor see nothin' neither,' he said grumpily. 'Where the hell are they?'

It was well past noon, and the sun was declining. Carnigan gave a deep, unhappy sigh.

'You know, O'Hara, this is the second time in three

70

days I bin forted up on a hot afternoon with Injuns after my hair.'

There was a snort of amusement.

'Thought it was kinda purty my own self,' O'Hara told him.

And suddenly the Apaches were upon them.

Carnigan found himself facing a yelling Indian who seemed to have jumped right up to the top of the rock in one bound. He heard O'Hara's carbine banging regularly, then the man's pistol.

The Apache kicked Carnigan's Henry to one side and reached for his eyes with clawed fingers.

Carnigan rolled desperately, pulling the rifle with him, escaping from the falling body of the Indian only by a sharp wriggle which threw him off the top of the boulder. The fall drove the wind out of him, and he lay for a second incapable of movement. Above him he saw the outline of the Indian, spread-eagled against the sky, and dropping towards him.

He rolled and rolled again, finding himself beneath the hoofs of his own horse, seeing the Apache stabbing at him with a knife.

Bright pictures were flickering in his mind. The Apache's extraordinarily broad face, nearly as wide as it was deep. The man's thin drawn lips pulled back in a snarl of impatience as he reached out with his knife.

Amazingly, the rifle was still in Carnigan's hands. As he rolled for the third time, the Apache changed his angle of attack and ran his chest right against the muzzle.

For a frozen split second, Indian and white man looked into one another's eyes, and then Carnigan pulled the trigger.

The shot was curiously muffled, and blood from the wound splashed into Carnigan's face. He thrust the Indian away from him and turned to see two Apaches closing on O'Hara.

Working the lever of the rifle, he shot into one of the men and turned towards the other. As he did so, out of the corner of his eye, he was aware of a horseman rounding the boulder, and there was another outburst of firing.

Abruptly, it was all over.

Blake and his troopers sat on blowing horses, and reloaded smoking weapons. Of the Apaches, only the two dead were left.

O'Hara sat with his back against the rock, and coughed weakly. Blood ran from his mouth as he did so. There was a lance through his chest, and the tip had broken off against the rock.

Carnigan hunkered down next to him and pulled the man's shirt away from the base of the lance. O'Hara's eyes met his with perfect understanding.

'Ain't nobody never recovered from a lung wound,' the big sergeant said. 'Don't bother pullin' out the lance. At least it plugs the hole for a while.'

'I got one of them,' Carnigan told him. O'Hara shook his head and coughed again.

'You got the wrong goddam one,' he protested. 'The one you shot was only *goin'* to stick me. The one who got away already had.'

He gave a death's head grin.

'At least I got the laugh on him. Bastard lost his goddamn lance!'

His laughter turned into a cough, the cough to a choking, and the blood came from his mouth in a torrent. As Blake leaned over him, the life oozed out of O'Hara, and he turned his face to the rock.

'And where the hell,' Carnigan asked the shocked officer, 'were you when the chips were down?'

FIVE

High on the shoulder of the mountain above them, Reno Styles put his binoculars back into his saddle-bag, and turned to smile at the girl who rode just behind him.

'Another one down. Only a dozen to go, now,' he told her and his smile widened as he saw her eyes fill with sadness.

Brinsley pushed his horse forward until it crowded the girl on the narrow ledge which skirted the brow of the mountain.

'They got Carnigan?' he demanded.

'Too far to tell. They're diggin' a hole to plant one of 'em, anyways,' Reno told him. He looked at the little man curiously.

'Who's so all-fired worried about Carnigan, anyway? I'd a thought you'd be glad to see him down,' he said.

Brinsley showed his teeth in the savage grin.

'I want to down him my own self,' he said. 'I want to see him dead, I want to put him in the ground where

74

I can lay a big rock on top of him.'

'What's the big deal?' asked Donner, whose horse was blocked by the bunch on the trail ahead. Natchez, sitting in the van of the party, chuckled deep in his throat.

'Brinsley ees more afraid of Carnigan than of any,' he sniggered. 'That ees the reason!'

In a flash, the gunman's pistol was in his hand. Only a quick downward slash from Reno's quirt prevented him from shooting. The Mexican had turned his horse slightly, and it revealed that his own gun was out and cocked, and pointed unwaveringly at Brinsley.

For a second, death hung above the group like a waiting vulture.

'Back off! Back off, damn you!'

Styles's lips were drawn back from his teeth in a bloodless line. His black eyes were wide and staring and his own hand was on the butt of his gun.

'Put that gun away, or I'll shoot you dead, Brin!' he said. 'I mean it!'

Brinsley knew he did mean it and the fire slowly ebbed from his eyes. He lowered his head and the pawl clicked as he uncocked the revolver and eased it back into his holster. But Styles had not missed the calculation in those flat, resentful eyes before the hat brim veiled them. Brinsley would kill him if he had the chance.

The girl allowed herself to breathe again, but only in shallow, hasty breaths. Rarely had she seen speed like it.

Styles noticed her heaving bosom, and grinned again, losing his own tension.

'Fast, ain't he?' he asked mockingly. 'Fastest thing on two legs, he reckons.'

Brinsley's snag tooth reappeared at the praise.

'Ain't seen nobody to beat me,' he said with satisfaction. 'Nobody come near me, though there's been plenty tried!'

Donner called again from behind. 'What's goin' on up there? We blocked ahead, or somethin'?'

'Naw, nothin',' Reno pulled the horse round and let it lead on up the trail. 'Nothin' atall! Keep an eye on the girl, Brin. I'm goin' ahead with Natchez to scout the top end. Ain't been up here for a year or more, I don't want to get trapped if she's fallen away, up ahead.'

Natchez allowed him past and fell in behind, holstering his own gun. He gave Brinsley a long, thoughtful glance, though. For his money, he had beaten Brinsley to the draw although all the others' eyes had been on the gunman, and not on Natchez, and he was sure none of the others had noticed.

It was a matter to be remembered, though, if there should come a showdown later on. And he was sure there would be, sooner or later.

He let Styles lead on up the trail. There were piñon pines here, clinging to the rocks, and some scrubby bushes hanging precariously to the few pockets of thin soil, but little other vegetation, and the mountain's bones showed through in the dark, red colours of the range, striped here and there with pale cream and green.

It was cold here and with the night it would get colder. They were high, more than 5,000 feet, and down in the foothills the night was already painting the rocks and trees dark shades of shadow. Up here, though, the dying sun still picked out the rocks, and the moving was easy enough.

Ahead the trail turned away from the precipice and entered a narrow defile, climbing steeply still and turning out of sight. The entrance to the defile was shrouded by the clump of small trees, and higher up he could see the tops of more.

'That's where we'll camp,' Styles said, and pointed. Natchez looked at him curiously. Ever since he had first met Reno, Natchez had been impressed by the man's careful planning.

Every job they had done, every raid they had carried out had been thought out beforehand with meticulous attention to detail, and a ruthlessness worthy of a great campaigner.

Natchez was used to a life in which events shaped him, rather than the other way around. At first, the Mexican had been amused by Styles's attention to detail, then puzzled and finally awed by it.

The man was utterly ruthless when it came to Indians. He slaughtered with a methodical and solemn intensity, men, women and children. His lack of passion disturbed even the callous Mexican.

Natchez had heard Donner remark that Reno had

lost his own family to an Indian raid, though Reno never talked about his past, save to comment on knowledge he had acquired.

It was probably true. The tale was common enough, after all. Many a homesteader or small rancher had returned to a smoking pile of ruins, to find his wife raped and tortured, his children murdered, his cattle butchered.

Such a man was left with literally nothing. Nothing, that was, except an undying hatred for the ones who had done this thing.

It was hardly surprising that such men often turned their rage and hurt against the next Indians they came across, whether they had anything to do with the outrage or not. The Indians, unsurprisingly, responded in kind and the whole business simply went on repeating itself.

Natchez could see nothing wrong in this. He had grown up in a country which offered $100 for a male Apache scalp, $50 for a female and $30 for a child. He did not think of Indians as people at all. Merely as animals worth more dead than alive and certainly a great deal safer.

'What is it with Brinsley, you reckon?' Reno rolled himself a cigarette and tossed the sack of makings to the Mexican.

'He afraid. He afraid of Carnigan,' Natchez said with a shrug.

His fingers worked deftly, making a cigarette paper into a little trough, tapping in the filling tobacco, licking the paper along its upper edge and twisting the end to seal the cigarette.

Reno flicked a match on his fingernail and lighted both his smoke and Natchez's.

'I dunno,' he said. 'I ain't seen Brin afeared of any man or animal, come to that. Little rooster's full of hisself, o' course, so how come he's frit o' Carnigan?'

'You know anything about Carnigan?' Natchez asked him, cocking an eyebrow. Reno shook his head. 'What I heard, he's a drifter. Done some scoutin'. Was in Mexico, tamed a town. No slouch, but I heard the same thing about a bunch o' guys, and it didn't make them real special.'

The Mexican looked around the visible skyline carefully as he talked, but he hooked a knee over the saddle horn and tipped the big sombrero back onto his shoulders.

'I fight with Carnigan, one time,' he said. 'Back in the Sonora, down in the Sierra Madre, you know? Down there the Apache run to get away from the soldiers up in Arizona. He was a *coronel*, a colonel of cavalry. Good soldier, lost few men. Good tracker. Hard, fast, nobody's fool. You know?'

Reno nodded and drew deeply on his cigarette, hiding the burning end in the palm of his hand so that it could not be seen from the distance. In the dusk in the mountains, a bright-burning brand can be seen for a surprising distance.

'We were having trouble with the Apache again. Chiricahuas. Mountain Apache, the worst. They were running from the cavalry and they cross the border and start raiding down there, holed up in the mountains, raiding down into the rancheros. Kill cattle, steal mules, women. They were gettin' ready to hole up for the winter.'

He shook his head, his eyes busy on the country he could see. It was getting dark faster now. The cool of the evening was turning into the cold of the night, and they were still not in their night camp. Maybe Reno did not want him to see the trail to it clearly.

'It was a bad campaign,' he said. 'The men were not happy. The pay was held up, of course. The pay was always held up. So were the rations, and the ammunition. We had bullets, though. Carnigan always found ammunition.

'The orders came to make a sweep, high up in the hills. Where the Chiricahua had their stronghold. We were on low rations, but the peons, the villagers, they always had food somewhere.

'We had a *teniente* called Baca. Julio Baca. He was mean, a bad man with the women. I think he was part Indian himself. He liked to hurt them, and he was good at it. I theenk maybe Brinsley is a leetle like him.'

Reno noticed that as he warmed to his story, the Mexican's accent came and went. He suspected that Natchez could speak without an accent if he wished, and wondered what else the man was hiding.

'There was a girl in the village. A pretty thing, and her father and mother had the best house there. Not much, you understand, just less of a hovel than the

80

others. Baca decided they had food and maybe even gold. Maybe they had.

'He took the girl into a barn and tried to make her tell where the food was hidden. She was screaming very much and for a long time. The *sargento* tried to stop him, but Baca beat him and went back to the girl.'

He was silent while his mind went back to the day. The *coronel* had come back to the village leading an exhausted patrol, one man across his saddle and another with bandages on.

He heard the girl's cries, and rode straight into the barn, not bothering to dismount.

'He dragged Baca out by his hair, and drew his sword. They called it a duel, afterwards, but it was not a duel. It was slaughter. Carnigan, he cut Baca into pieces.'

He stubbed out his cigarette against his boot heel and dropped the dead end into his pocket.

'He did it slowly. He cut him a little at a time until he was covered in blood. His uniform was so bad, he look as though he had been making love to a cactus. You could wring the blood from it afterwards like a dishcloth. At the end, Baca went to his knees and begged for mercy. Cried like a child.'

Reno watched him, fascinated. It was the first time Natchez had ever revealed anything of his own past at all.

'And did Carnigan spare him?'

Natchez laughed. 'No. He cut off his head with one

81

stroke – *fsst*, just like that! He cleaned his sword on
Baca's shirt and said: "Throw that offal on the
midden!" '

'And did you?'

'Are you serious? Of course we did. Very queeck.
After that, no discipline problem of any kind. We were
more afraid of him than we were of any man in the
world, except maybe Cochise. And Cochise is not on
my trail at this moment!'

Reno recalled the Indians he had seen through his
field glasses running from the cavalry below. They had
fled up the mountains.

Towards Reno and his party.

'I wouldn't be sure of that, *amigo*,' he told Natchez'
retreating back, as they rode into the now dark defile
to find their campsite.

A rattle of a dislodged stone from the canyon
behind them reminded him that the rest of the gang
was only a little way behind, and by now in easy
earshot of the leaders.

It had been in Reno's mind to kill the Mexican
while they were up the trail, and out of sight of the
rest. He had no intention of sharing the gold from the
Army payroll with any of his comrades, and the girl
was far too good to share.

From the moment he had planned the robbery, he
had planned also to rid himself of the men who rode
with him. They had served their purpose, and with this
big haul, that purpose was ended.

Reno Styles was not his real name, of course. He

planned, when this was all over, to return to his former life. It had been a long time now since he had sat down to a properly laid table for a meal, slept in a bed with sheets, or worn clothes which were not rough woollen shirts and jeans.

In banks to the east of here there were accounts in different names known only to him, where he had salted away the proceeds of his carefully-planned life of crime.

He had cheated his partners and everybody else with whom he had come into contact, simply to finance his dream. It was a dream he had nurtured all his life, and now he was ready to bring it to fruition.

The dream of being a respected, respectable man.

Reno saw himself in a large house, with a carriage and horses, and servants to look after them. He saw himself wearing fine body-linen and handmade suits.

He knew exactly where he would live, because he had his roots in that community. It was a community which had rejected him, and he would force them all to accept him back. Money was the key to unlock that particular door, and this haul at last gave him enough of it.

Reno was a son of the manse. His father had been a travelling preacher with hell fire in his mouth and a leather belt in the hand which did not hold the Bible. The belt was to teach his son and his persecuted, hard working wife respect for both God and His servant here on earth.

Rank was very important to such a man, and the preacher had that, too, with a commission in the local militia. Granted, he had raised the militia himself, and issued his own commission, but he was an officer nevertheless, and the men followed him.

When Reno was little more than a child he had been taken by his father to raid a local Indian village.

The Indians were not troublesome, but they were indolent, sometimes drunk, and they regarded the preacher and his flock with a kind of amused tolerance which infuriated him.

Anyway, they were Indians. What need for an excuse to 'cleanse' the country of them?

The raid turned into a massacre. Over a hundred Indians, most of them women, children and the elderly, had been slaughtered by the troopers. His father had ridden back and forth, ordering the deaths of the children personally.

'Nits grow into lice!' he kept saying, until even his half trained troopers turned from the butchery in disgust at both him and themselves.

His father had been dismissed from the military, his command dispersed, and a new regular unit posted into the district to keep order. The commanding officer and the local Indian agent did their best to bring charges against the preacher.

Eventually, as the little town grew into a thriving community, the townsfolk deserted his church, and he took more and more to the Bible and the bottle. His rages became more and more violent.

In the end, he turned, one dreadful night, upon first his wife and then his son.

It was a fatal mistake, for in the intervening years the dazed youth who had watched the butchery of the Indian children had grown into a gangling but powerful adolescent.

He tore the belt from his father's grasp, knocked him down and administered a beating with the big brass buckle which appalled even the local doctor when he was called to examine the body. He testified that the preacher had died from inhaling his own vomit while unconscious and drunk, but the community of Little Falls had drawn its own conclusions, and a couple of local men with shotguns called round to see the widow and orphan that night.

'You can stay and welcome,' the preacher's widow had been told, sympathetically. 'We need a schoolteacher, and the kids like you.'

Reno, however, was the boy who had murdered his father, and however much the community might understand the reason, it was not ready to shelter an unnatural killer in its midst.

Besides, there was hardly a man in the community who had not at some time or other taken a drink too many, or raised his hand to his children in a moment of wrath. They did not want a known patricide in their bosom, provoking who knew what dangerous thoughts among their young.

Reno was told firmly to go.

That night, he took the family horse and what money he could find and rode away to make his living the only way he had ever been taught - by beating out

85

of anybody who was weaker than he.

Curiously, the Little Falls Indian affair had left him with an abiding hatred of Indians. He killed them wherever he found them with a ferocious intensity. He took their scalps to sell. And he looked upon the work as good and cleansing.

He despised weakness and took advantage of it wherever he could. He mistook compassion and decency for weakness often, and was always outraged when decent men turned out to be neither cowardly nor weak, and indeed when provoked, capable of cloaking their compassion, and running him out of town, which in his early years they often did.

He also hated men who were stronger than he. For this reason if for no other, he hated Carnigan, recognizing in him the inner confidence and strength which he, Reno, felt he lacked. Like Brinsley, he regretted not killing the man when he first met him at Antelope Rock, or later in the trading post.

But, he told himself as they made their camp in a shallow cave halfway up the narrow pass, that could be put right very shortly.

'Kill Carnigan, and they'll lose us,' Brinsley said as they sat around the fire. 'Kill Carnigan and we got it made high, wild and free!'

Mart Donner hunkered over the little tepee of sticks over which he was frying bacon in a frying-pan. A pot of beans bubbled at the side of the fire and there was coffee sitting in the embers.

'You kill him,' he said over his shoulder. 'Me, I don't want no part of that man. He's an old cata-mount, and there ain't no part of that 'un that ain't barbed wire, cactus thorns and pure pizen.'

He dragged a thick slice of bacon on to a tin plate, added beans and held it out to the woman. She was sitting back against the wall, a blanket over her legs and another round her shoulders, nursing a tin cup of coffee which was too hot to put to her lips.

'Give it here!' Reno reached out and passed it to her, and she took hold of it with one hand, while she balanced the coffee with the other. Briefly, she considered throwing the near-boiling coffee in his face, but instantly dismissed the idea. The longer they thought of her as weak and compliant, the more chance she would have of making a break for it later.

Besides, if she did escape from Reno, there were the three others who could catch her easily, and Reno was all that was keeping them from her at the moment, she knew. And outside that entrance there were the rocks, the mountains and the bitter cold. Who knew how far back the soldiers were – and who knew where the Indians were, either.

She ate the food, she drank the coffee and she checked that the little knife which her father had given her to tuck into the top of her boot was still in place. It was very sharp, and if the worst came to the worst, she would make sure they were all marked in one way or another.

They had arrived here in the moments between

sundown and full dark, climbing the thin eyebrow of trail which brought them out of the canyon and on to the flat, empty space in front of the cave. There were pines and scrub here, and the defile led on upwards at the far side of the little space.

From below, as Reno said, it was invisible unless a man knew what to look for. There was room for the horses to stand, picketed on a line. And within the cave itself, the ashes of many fires showed it had sheltered generations of travellers. The cleft at the back which was smoke stained from many years before, acted as a chimney which would dispel the smoke before it reached the open air.

'Found an old sword back there, one time,' Reno commented when Donner remarked on the age of the little fireplace neatly pieced together from fallen stones.

'Broke below the hilt, she was. Spanish, I reckon. Been there a whole heap of years from the looks of her. Left by some of the old soldiers who came here with the old Spanish pioneers, I guess.'

'What happened to it?' Brinsley was curious.

'Disappeared by the next time I come. Some pilgrim taken it along to sell, I guess. Should 'a thought of it myself, maybe. Or maybe an Indian took it to make hisself a knife. Surprised it lasted so long, but it was pretty well hid. Just behind the fire, there.'

He pointed, and they all stared, except Natchez. He was sitting behind a rock in the cave entrance, a plate of food on his knee, staring out at the dark.

'See anything?' said Donner.

The Mexican shook his head, but he did not make the mistake of looking back into the cave, where the light of the fire would have destroyed his night vision. He was watching the trail where it came up the defile through the trees. He could see the dark mass of the trees, and the longer he stared, the less he saw.

'You reckon they'd risk it in the night? Come upon us in the dark?' said Brinsley.

Reno shook his head.

'Hell, no,' he said. 'They couldn't come up that eyebrow trail in the dark. They'll have camped down in the canyon. Be up here first light, I reckon. I got a plan to hold 'em up, though.'

He cleared a patch of sand with a twig and brushed it flat with his hat brim.

'Trail comes around the mountain round about here,' he said, scratching with the twig. Brinsley leaned closer to see and Donner put down the pan and leaned closer.

'But the trail we take tomorrow doubles back over the top of 'em. There's one that goes out of the top of the gulch here, and another goes up behind the trees over there, and doubles back, but a couple of hundred feet further up.

'Mountain leans back round about here, and from the top trail you can see the lower trail. Wouldn't be no trick at all to pick off a man on the lower trail, and they ain't no other way to come up here. Think back this afternoon, and that low trail's too narrow to turn round.

'Hit the first man up, and the others'll have to back down out of sight, and a good shot can hit two or even three more, maybe. Maybe even the whole lot.'

Privately, he doubted it. Carnigan or that big sergeant – he was unaware that O'Hara was the man he had seen buried that afternoon – would see the danger of the exposed route, and send their men over it one at a time.

But he planned that, while Brinsley was waiting to pick off Carnigan, he would be making time with the girl and the money.

Natchez would have to be the first one to die, he calculated. The dark Mexican with the flat, passionless eyes disturbed him strangely. He had also not missed the fact that Natchez had beaten Brinsley to the draw that afternoon. A hair thin piece of timing, to be sure, but he had actually beaten the little gunman to it.

He was a killer, too, of a totally different type from Brinsley. Where the little man was quick and poisonous, like a spider, Natchez moved slowly and carefully until the moment came to strike, and then he killed with a speed and expertise which Reno both envied and feared.

The second to go would be Mart Donner. The thick-set man was passionless and thoughtlessly brutal. And he wanted the girl with an animal lust which was palpable whenever they stopped to rest.

The trick was going to be to keep them all off the girl tonight. While they felt secure and comfortable in their camp the lust would come to the surface, He would have to think of something to unsettle them, to keep them on edge and jumpy.

'We'll need a man on watch, though,' he said, as Natchez turned from the entrance and walked back into the cave to help himself to coffee from the pot.

'Why?' Donner's eyes were on the girl, who had finished eating and was gazing hopelessly into the fire.

Reno followed his gaze and cursed inwardly. It had started already. Donner's next thought would be the drink which was in Reno's saddle-bags. Once drunk, he would be unmanageable.

'Apaches,' he said, and was rewarded with a jerk of the head from Brinsley and Natchez.

'Injuns? Where?'

'Behind us. They may not catch up. But when the major come up to Carnigan and the other man, the Injuns run. And they run uphill. They's only one trail. They's between us and Carnigan,' he said.

Donner held out his coffee-cup without taking his eyes off the woman. The Mexican filled it, and did the same for Brinsley.

All three of them squatted there by the fire, watching her. Marion Crawshaw pulled the blankets closer round her shoulders and stared hopelessly into the fire. In the flickering light, the gold of her hair seemed to take on a life of its own.

'Throw some more fuel on to that fire,' said Reno, suddenly. 'Natchez – get back on watch. Apaches don't mind gettin' wet! What you thinkin' of?'

But he was too late. They were drinking, now, and

their thoughts were full of the woman. The lust filled the cave like a living thing.

Brinsley reached behind him and took wood from the pile of dry branches they had brought in with them. He heaped several on to the little blaze, making the flames leap higher, and filling the cave with a flickering yellow light.

Donner licked his lips.

'Come here, girl,' he said thickly.

Marion ignored him. She was a small figure, cocooned in her blankets against the night and their eyes.

Donner stood up and let his gunbelt drop.

'Iffen I have to come and get you, girl, I'll take my belt to you,' he said. 'There ain't no escape.'

Brinsley giggled, a high, almost feminine, sound.

'Maybe he'll take his belt to you anyways. Teach you some manners, you stuck up bitch!' he jeered.

Donner started across the cave, walking slowly and menacingly. His shadow, distorted monstrously by the fire, danced on the wall above her head.

'When I tell you to come, girl, you come quick!' he said. His low, gravel tones rolled in the smoky light. He reached down and took her by the hair, pulling her to her feet. The blankets fell away.

'Take 'em off!' He grabbed at the neck of her jacket, and ripped. The buttons showered to the ground but the material resisted his tearing hand, and he let go of her hair to use both hands. The lapels fell open, and Brinsley giggled again, an ugly sound.

'Bring 'er here where we can all see, Mart! Bring 'er to the fire!'

Donner dragged her across the cave to the full fire-light. His eyes were alight with lust and the firelight dancing on his face turned him into a bearded satyr.

Her face was twisted with pain and she fought against him wildly, kicking out. But her feet were muffled in the heavy riding skirt. He shook her and laughed as she gasped on a high-pitched note.

'You wanna kick? I'll help you!'

He grabbed at the waistband of her skirt, letting go of her hair again, and material gave with a heavy rending sound. The garment fell to the ground. She kicked again but the material around her ankles stopped her.

'Hey, you know somet'in? When I hit that major, her neck was open then! I theenk she sweet on heem,' Natchez called. 'Le's see what he was lookin' at!'

Donner put his hand in the neck of the blouse and this time the material ripped more easily. They stared at her heaving breasts, pushed high by the tight corset.

'Hey, that ol' major, he wasn't no fool!' shouted Brinsley. 'That there's worth lookin' at! Show us, Mart!'

But Donner had come up against the mysteries of feminine underwear. He released his hold on the girl to use both hands on the laces at the back of the garment, and she turned, quick as a wolf, and sank her teeth into his hand.

He swore and threw her off and she leaped for the

open. Brinsley caught her ankle and she measured her length on the floor.

Reno admitted to himself that there was nothing he could do. He had no desire to join in the rape of the girl, but he could not prevent it. There would, after all, be other girls, and other places, once he was away with the money.

Natchez was leaning against the wall, laughing, as Brinsley grabbed for the girl's wrists. She slashed her nails across his eyes, and blood showed where she had caught him. He swore, and raised one hand to cuff her.

'I'll show you, you little hellcat!' he swore. 'First I'll—'

'First, you'll die, if you don't keep still!' said Carnigan's voice pleasantly from the darkness outside. 'Heered once what they done to a couple of men took a woman into the woods down Telluride way. Put me clean off my breakfast, and even Cochise woulda been proud of it, the way they treated them old boys!'

It was as though ice had descended from the mountain and filled the cave. The people within it froze into position instantly. With no target to shoot at and no idea how many guns pointed into the cave, not one of the men dared reach for a gun.

Carnigan stepped into the firelight and put his back against the wall within the entrance.

'O' course, they ain't gonna need to be inventive with you boys. Cochise is goin' to get you first. What he can't think up ain't worth the tellin'. Not when you've et.'

Reno was the first to come out of it. He realized Carnigan was alone, and reached for his gun. Carnigan's hand came up and the Henry faced them over the fire.

'Don't even think about it,' Carnigan told him. 'Only reason any one of you is still alive is that across the top of this ridge, there's eight or ten Apaches camped. Right now, they's wet and they's miserable, and they's thinkin' how warm and cosy it is in here. Start shootin' and they're likely to think your attention done been distracted, and come runnin'.'

Brinsley had forgotten the girl. He was still caught in mid-stretch. His right hand was reaching for the girl's wrist and about as far from his gun as it could be and still remain attached to his body. Every instinct in his mean, dark soul screamed at him to draw – but every reasoning instinct screamed equally loudly for him to keep still.

'Miss Crawshaw, can you come over here without gettin' between me and the boys, thar?' said Carnigan.

Slowly, she pulled herself from under Brinsley and crawled round the fire, keeping her head low. She grabbed her skirt on the way and reached out for her jacket.

But Carnigan was planning a different course.

'On your feet, boys, and shuck them gunbelts,' he told Brinsley and Natchez. 'Do it slow and with your left hand and you could survive the night. Ain't guaranteein' anythin', though. You too, Reno. Get clever, get dead.'

Slowly and carefully Reno did as he was told. He was thinking wistfully of the Derringer in the top of his boot, but to get at it, he would have to pull up his trouser-leg and he was perfectly convinced Carnigan meant what he said.

'Iffen shootin' will bring them Apach', you would-n't risk it your own self,' said Brinsley, his eyes glinting. He was upright, now. His hand was close enough to the holster to take a chance, he reckoned.

The muzzle of the Henry did not waver one millimetre.

'If it's a choice between the Indians and you, I'll take my chances with Cochise,' Carnigan told him cheerfully. 'I ain't gettin shot by you to save my life from them. So I'll shoot you men first and take my chances.

'After all, I know Apaches. Mayhap my brother in law's out there with 'em. I got more brothers-in-law down in the Chiricahuas than a dog's got fleas, and that don't count uncles, aunts and cousins. How many Chiricahua scalps you took, you reckon, Brin?'

The little man paled. He and his partners were well known to the Apache. If there was the slightest chance of being captured, he would be best advised to turn his pistol on himself. Better a quick death than the protracted agony the Indians would have in store for him. He had seen men who had been caught by the Apache.

Carnigan watched the mental processes reflected in the gunman's face, and then he smiled. It was not a pretty smile, and Brinsley was reminded the lean scout had spent time with the Apaches. He swallowed hard and cursed himself for not taking his chances on the previous day when he first met Carnigan.

But, now that he put his mind to it, he could not recall one instant since Carnigan came down off the rock when the man was not on his guard. Even when he had been pinned to the floor by the weight of the wounded Kellerman, it had been touch and go whether Brinsley could actually have shot him without exposing himself to the risk of death.

He had heard of men who had survived more than ten bullet wounds, and still gone on fighting, and he had seen one man with five bullets in him still standing and firing back at his attackers. And killing two of them, as well, he recalled.

Carnigan surveyed Marion Crawshaw with a worried eye. The girl seemed to have come through her ordeal without being devastated by it, but how he was going to get her back over the ridge in the rain he did not know.

Outside, the rain was falling in sheets, and the rocks were slick and slippery. Her boots were unsuitable to the terrain, but there was little he could do about that. The clothes, however, he could change. Any attempt to cross the spine of rock in a skirt would be suicide.

'Miss Crawshaw,' he said, 'which o' these here men do you reckon is the cleanest?'

She goggled at him. 'What?'

'Which o' these here guys do you reckon is the least filthy, then?'

97

'I don't . . . why on earth are you asking me this?'

'On account of you're goin' to have to wear his pants,' said Carnigan grimly. 'Reno, I reckon you're the least dirty o' the bunch. Drop 'em!'

Reno looked amazed, and Carnigan gave him a lazy smile.

'Them jeans is comin' off you, dead or alive, Reno. You can take 'em off your own self, or I can drop you and take 'em off your body.

' 'Course, I'll have to kill the others, too. Choice is yourn.'

'Give them to him, Reno. We'll get even with him later,' Donner ground out. Reno slowly divested himself of his jeans, and stood, smouldering, in his long johns.

'Put on those . . . those things, when that beast has just taken them off? I'd rather die!' she snapped.

Carnigan sighed a long, hard sigh.

'Miss Crawshaw,' he said, 'I have had a long, hard day. A real hard day. I rode fifty mile. I clumb a mountain. I fought Apaches, and when the rain come instead of sitting by a nice, warm fire drinkin' coffee, I clumb all over this ridge to save you.

'Now, I don't know how women folks feel about that there same fate. I come across a few myself who tell me they favour it a million times better'n death.'

She snorted, but there was a hard, decisive look in his eye which made her keep her mouth closed.

'Any woman claims it is a worse fate than death at the hands of the Apache sure ain't seen one of their women prisoners after a few hours in the hands of half a dozen Chiricahua bucks. You sure ain't seen one, and you sure don't wanna see one. But all that is by the bye. You say you'd sooner die than wear them pants? I tell you iffen you don't put them pants on real quick you are surely goin' to die – and it will take you a long, long time, and you sure won't get bored. Now get dressed, dammit, woman and be quick about it!'

She shot him a look compounded of sheer amazement and outrage, but her common sense prevailed, and, muttering, she snatched the jeans, forced them over her boots and buttoned them around her waist.

They fitted her around the hips a good deal more tightly than the stringy outlaw, he noticed.

'Good,' Carnigan told her. 'Now pick yourself a coat. A leather one would be good.'

She wrinkled her nose at Brinsley's coat, and settled once again for Reno's.

'That's as good as we're goin' to get,' said Carnigan. 'Now if you'll step out on the ledge, ma'am, we'll be on our way.'

Marion Crawshaw stepped out into the rain, looked up at the weeping sky and returned to take the hat from Brinsley's saddle horn.

Brinsley watched her with eyes like a rattlesnake.

'It's goodbye for now, gel,' he hissed. 'But next time I see you, we'll take up where we left off, you and me. And I'll kill you after!'

She paused as she turned away, looked him in the eye and swung a small, balled fist in a fast arc. It smashed into Brinsley's mouth with surprising force, splitting his lips against his teeth and sending him backwards over his saddle with its unexpected power.

'That's for laying your dirty hands on me,' she said clearly. 'Next time, I'll break your nose for you. You won't have three friends to protect you then!'

The astounded men stared dumbfounded at her retreating figure as she stepped out into the wet darkness.

Carnigan gave a surprised bark of laughter.

'That's goin' to make good tellin' in the Long Branch, Brin,' he said. 'Tale like that'll keep them laughin' from Santa Fe to Tombstone and back.

'Now, fellers, face down on the floor, hands behind your heads, and the first one to stick his head out the entrance gets it blowed off!'

He was gone before they could look up. Outside there was the relentless drumming of the raindrops, and nothing else broke the silence.

SIX

Natchez was the first to break the silence. He went to the opening and looked out carefully. Below he could heard the rushing of the water, running off the rocky sides of the mountain and filling the gorge.

He knew what it meant, but to be certain, he pulled on his serape, jammed his hat over his eyes, and walked down the trail to stare at the flood. He knew, then, where the pair had gone, that they had gone over the mountain above and behind him.

When he returned to the cave, Reno was searching through his saddle bags and cursing vividly.

'Got some spare jeans in one o' these,' he said when Brinsley asked. 'And I'm sure goin' to need 'em, while we chase them two down the hill.'

Natchez hunkered down by the fire and fed it from the wood which had been scattered in the struggle with the girl. The flames leaped up, illuminating his face.

'Nobody goin' to chase them tonight,' he said. 'That for sure, *hombre*.'

'Huh?' Brinsley stared at him. 'What d'you mean? 'Course we got to ketch 'em. They can'ta gone far in this!'

The Mexican shook his head. 'No matter how far, you never fin' them tonight. They go up and over the mountain. No tracks, and eef there were, they would be wipe' out by the rain.

'You go wanderin' over the mountain tonight in the rain, what you gonna fin' is Apaches. They be real please to see you, Brin!'

He gave Brinsley a friendly grin.

'Worse still, maybe you fin' that leetle *señorita*. Nex' time, mebbe she break your nose for you, like she say!'

He broke off and the grin disappeared as Brinsley whipped a knife from his boot and slashed at him over the fire. The little man was spitting with rage as Donner grabbed him from behind, shaking with laughter.

'Lay off, Mex,' he sniggered. 'Can't you see pore Brin's all tuckered out, fightin' that strappin' big girl? Leave him alone!'

It took Reno to calm the situation with his spare Colt, before they were sitting once again around their fire. Brinsley winced as the whisky bit into his split lip. But his rage and humiliation had turned into a smouldering hatred for the girl.

'I ain't kiddin',' he snarled when Donner began to rib him again. 'When I get through with that bitch, she'll come crawlin'! Crawlin'!'

Reno watched him across the flames with hooded

102

eyes. The time to go, he told himself, was just before dawn.

The water in the canyon would not subside much before midday . But it did mean the soldiers could not get to them by the trail until at least then. But there was a path which led to the top of the rocky ridge behind the cave, and up which a horse might be led. It was, likely as not, the way Carnigan had reached them. But to attain the top of the rimrock, he must have left the soldiers before the rain had started.

How he had got past the cave with Natchez on guard, Reno neither knew nor at this time cared.

But, he reasoned, that meant that Carnigan could not rejoin the soldiers. He must be up ahead somewhere and, burdened with the girl, he would not be making good time.

It was possible that when Reno and the others moved out in the dawn, they would overrun the fugitives.

Always supposing they did not run, instead, into the Apaches.

Quite apart from the physical dangers he faced, Carnigan was deeply worried. The Apache should not in fact be out at all, and certainly not in this area at this time.

The woman ahead had stopped, leaning against a rock and breathing in sobbing gasps. Carnigan hauled himself up alongside her and tapped her shoulder.

'Sorry, Miss Crawshaw, but we have to go on,' he

said quietly. 'If Reno and his men were not after us, the Indians may be. We have to be off this mountainside by daylight, no matter what.'

She raised her head and stared dully at him in the gloom. He could see only her eye sockets, deeply shadowed, and the outline of her face under the broad hat, but she nodded, and forced herself forward. On the narrow trail, just putting one foot in front of another, was a hazard, but they progressed.

Their progress was made possible at all only by Carnigan's very clear mental picture of the ground they were covering.

Ahead, the trail led over the bulk of the mountain to where the true rock stopped and the snowline began. To their right, the peaks soared, white and majestic. To their left, the land fell away to the tree-line in a succession of ridges and canyons which made any kind of progress well nigh impossible. A man might go up or down, but traversing the mountainside was prevented by its ribs.

It was in one of these canyons that Reno and his men now huddled round their fire. They were separated from the Apache by a rocky ridge, along the backbone of which Carnigan and the girl were presently clambering.

At the top end of the ridge Carnigan's horse was waiting, sheltered from the weather by an overhang, and ground-hitched only by his trailing reins. The horse with its supplies was Carnigan's immediate aim. Once they had got there, they would have completed the first stage of their escape.

There would remain the problem of staying out of the hands of their enemies. Carnigan was as aware as Natchez that the Major and his depleted command were now completely cut off from them by the flooded canyon and the Indians.

He and the woman were on their own, with only one horse between them. The woman would have to ride the horse, because she was almost at the end of her tether, and he could call on depths of strength she did not have. This meant that even when they did have the horse, their speed would be restricted to what Carnigan could do on foot. And he, too, had just spent an exhausting twenty-four hours.

She, on the other hand, had passed forty eight exhausting hours. While he slept last night, she had been on the move with her captors. The drain on her nerves of the thought of certain rape and probable murder must have been pitiless.

The woman stopped again and he almost bumped into her. He turned her face to him and even in the dim light he was shocked at the exhaustion he could see.

He let her rest for a few minutes while he refilled his canteen from a rainy run-off, and made her drink from her cupped hands. The water contained sand and grit, but it was essentially clean, and while it was raining, they might as well stockpile as much water as they could.

Some time during the climb the rain stopped.

During one of their increasingly frequent rest periods, Carnigan, looking up, could see that the clouds were breaking, and fingers of starlight were visible. In their black world, the cobweb brightness of the stars lay visible over the rocks, reflected in the rain.

It was not the beauty which delighted him but the fact that instead of moving by feel and stumble, he could make better time. There were brief periods even of moonlight, now.

But if Carnigan could move faster, so could Reno. He could not climb the precipitous path Carnigan and the girl were taking, but he could, if he was careful, ride his horse up by a wider-swinging trail and arrive at the same point.

Desperate, he would do it. Carnigan knew that he would, and the thought lent an extra urgency to his pace.

He slid down the last steep pitch of the trail, bumping into the woman who was clawing her way along ahead of him. He heard his horse shift its feet and blow gently through its nostrils at him in the dark.

For a moment, he allowed himself to lean against the rock and pant, but only for a moment. The horse shifted again, and he realized it was nervous. It must be the woman: the horse was unfamiliar with her scent, and he could not rely on the animal to stand while he loaded her into the saddle.

He reached for the reins and stopped when the horse tossed its head and stepped away from him. The combination of the smells of the looted jeans and

106

jacket and the unfamiliar woman-smell behind it, he supposed.

He caught the reins, pushed the woman into the saddle and climbed up behind her. They still had a little way to climb before they could cross over into the next gorge and travel down it and into the valley he had been thinking of for years as 'Carnigan's Claim'.

Alternately riding and walking, he took the horse over the rock ridge, into the gorge, skirting the rocks and the outstretched buttresses of the walls.

He could not understand the creature's increasing nervousness, however. It became increasingly skittish, lunging against the reins from time to time. He could feel it quivering under him, and eventually he stopped and swung down again, leaving the reins in the hands of the woman.

The grulla was by all accounts used to the mountains. Its owner was a renowned mountain man so the altitude could not be disturbing it.

But when he remounted, its nerves took over, and it danced skittishly, laying its ears back and rolling its eyes.

A deadfall blocked the trail ahead, a nightmare of spiky branches and clawing twigs. He gave the reins to the woman again, and went forward to find a way round the barrier.

He had broken away the top section and cut back the worst of the branches to make a path round the end of it when the woman hissed at him.

Immediately, he went to her. She was pointing back down the defile.

'I thought I heard something move back there,' she said in a low voice.

'Men? How many?'

'I don't know. Just a stone clicked. It may have been one we dislodged coming up.'

He climbed into the saddle behind her, and threw the horse at the gap. For a moment, it hung back, wary of the sharp branches. Then they were past with a lunge, and he pushed the horse as fast as he dared, urging it up the rough path.

'What on earth is behind us?' whispered the woman shrilly.

He was in the act of dismounting to lead the horse again when he heard the clatter of hoofs behind them in the canyon. He slammed himself back into the saddle to urge the tired grulla into a run.

The time for stealth was long past now. He was on the run.

The horse responded gamely, almost with gratitude, and produced from somewhere a spurt of speed to run itself out of the trap.

From behind came a whoop, and he heard the following horses speed up as well, rattling up the defile in a welter of noise.

The Apaches were up and around at last.

He pulled the horse to its haunches, and slipped off its back, pulling the Henry with him, then slapped the animal on the rump. With a galvanized leap it took the woman on up the canyon, out of harm's way.

Carnigan sighted with exquisite care on the gap he

had created between the top of the deadfall and the canyon wall, and as the first Apache showed in the opening, squeezed the trigger gently. The rifle thumped into his shoulder, and the Indian dropped.

A second shot dropped the pony in the gap, and a third skinned the top of the head of the next man along. The sound of approaching horses stopped.

Carnigan grinned with relief and turned to run after the fleeing woman, only to find her standing behind the next rock, the grulla's reins tied to her wrist, and the pistol he had taken from Reno balanced across her forearm. The horse, blown but recovering, had calmed down now.

'Thought I told you to ride on!' he panted as he came round the rock and took the reins from her.

'I thought you needed backing up,' she said coolly. 'I'm a soldier's daughter. I cut my teeth on a Navy Remington, and I know enough to save the last bullet for myself.'

Carnigan looked down on the top of her purloined hat with increasing respect. He had come to rescue a spoiled army brat and found himself holding a bobcat.

The grulla scrambled over a last pile of detritus from the mountain above and out of the gorge on to a small plateau strewn with rubble and boulders. At the other side of the plateau, a larger gorge plunged down the mountainside.

The larger gorge split as it descended into a number of smaller gorges. And to his right, there was a forbidding slope of shale which led to the mouth of Hand-me-Down Pass which led to the valley he sought.

He pulled up and let the horse breathe.

The day was fully advanced, now, and the sun was bright on his face as he stood at the edge of the plateau and looked around. He heard the woman dismount from the grulla and walk to join him.

'Did we lose them?' she said.

He shrugged. 'You don't ever lose Apaches completely,' he said. 'It just takes them more time to find the trail again, sometimes.'

'But will they come after us?'

'Hard to say. Probably yes. Certainly if they knew you were a woman, but I doubt they do. They ain't seen you in woman's clothes and they was too far off to make out anything but the clothes. But Indians is notional folk. Maybe they'll decide we're bad medicine for 'em. Indians'll do that. Or maybe they'll figure they spent enough lives chasin' us, and just go on home, or find someone else to kill.'

While he was talking, he was rolling a cigarette, and as he finished, he lighted it with a match scratched on a rock.

He flicked a glance at her before he went to studying the countryside again. After a while, he went to the horse and fished around in the saddle bags until he came up with a pair of very battered binoculars.

'Had me a fine pair of glasses, ones I took off an officer in the War Between the States,' he said. 'Them goddamn Utes got those.'

110

He fiddled with the focus wheel for a time, and then grunted with satisfaction.

'These uns of Con Kellerman's don't work quite as well,' he said. 'But they do work.'

She watched him, wondering.

'This here's Hand-me-Down Pass,' he told her, pointing down the valley towards the far mountains. 'It's on the side of this mountain, and it's on the saddle of that one over there. Sort of like it's been handed down to the other mountain, like.'

He handed her the binoculars. 'Look down the line of the pass a bit, to where an old bald knob of rock sticks out, on the right.'

She peered through the glasses until she had found the landmark he described.

'To the side of that knob there's a kind of a hanging valley. A deep V shape in the side of the canyon,' he said.

She nodded, mystified. 'Why are you telling me all this?'

'In case I don't make it,' he said. 'You'll know what to look for. If I stay back, or we get split any time, you make for that valley. You get into the mouth there and you'll find a game trail wanders along the left hand wall of her.'

He hunkered down on his heels and started feeding shells from his cartridge belt into the Henry.

'Foller that trail, and you'll find it opens into a basin, about ten mile or so along. Right pretty place, with a lake in the bottom, and a waterfall comes down

111

from the high snows. To the side of the waterfall they's a cabin, with supplies and a corral.

'Stay there until I come for you. Or if I don't come, leave it a few days until you reckon the pursuit's left the mountains, and make your way back down the pass here to the foot. They's a town down there called Placerville. They'll telegraph your Daddy from there.'

He stood up again, and gave her a level look.

'If you hear I'm dead, you can have that there cabin and that valley for your own. There's about twenty head of the finest horses in Colorado down there, and a few cattle. But the whole valley's deeded to me. Just so long as you look after them horses and live in that there cabin for a time or two.'

She looked at him out of giant eyes.

'You're giving me your home?' she said. 'Just like that?'

He shrugged. 'Why not? Ain't got nobody else to leave 'er to. Thought about marriage once in a while, but this here country's hell on women and horses, and I had my hands full looking after the stock.'

He made a stirrup, completely unnecessarily, with his hands.

'Go on, mount up,' he said gruffly. 'Git movin'! I'll be along later.'

The last she saw of him as the grulla stepped down the shale slope was the flat, black hat disappearing down the gorge up which they had recently come.

SEVEN

Down in the confined air of the gorge, the heat had not yet begun to build up, and water was certainly no problem. After the storm of the night before there were puddles and miniature waterways all over the floor of the canyon.

Carnigan picked himself a rock at his leisure, and hunkered down behind it, devoting his waiting time to rolling himself a succession of coffin nail cigarettes which he laid in a groove along the top of the slab.

He had a ready-made loophole along one side of the rock, and a tiny tunnel on the other which looked straight down the throat of the canyon, and would be impossible to hit from below.

There was a series of possibilities open to his pursuers. The Apaches, he was convinced, would simply follow doggedly along his trail until they caught up with him. There would be a pitched battle, and at some point they would either kill him or decide the price of doing so was too high, and fade away into the rocks.

It still bothered him that these Apaches were so far

north. To get to the Uncompahgres they would have had to cross the territory of at least three other tribes, all of them potentially hostile to the Apache, and that meant a singleness of purpose generally devoted only to a blood feud.

He made sure the wind was blowing up the canyon, and would carry his smoke away from the Indians and out on to the mountain, before he lit the first of his cigarettes and settled to a careful examination of the entrance of the gorge below and the sides immediately above his position.

First, he mentally divided the terrain into sections marked with obvious features. A fallen tree. A vertical crack in the rocks. A bunch of curious bushes. He studied each section with care, not moving to the next until he had memorized the previous one.

There was a quirk of amusement in his mind as he remembered the sinewy youth who had loftily imparted this bit of desert law to him.

'Making friends with the land,' Walks Far Quickly had called it. 'For will a friend betray a friend? Only when a man knows the land as a friend can he expect it to give him its secrets.'

It was a long winded way of saying if you studied the terrain, you would more easily see any changes.

Long winded, but it sure stuck in the mind.

Sooner or later the Apaches would be coming up that slope – though they sure were taking their time about it, he thought, with a twinge of anxiety – and he would be ready for them.

He also devoted some time to the mouth of the canyon up which the Reno party should come, if they decided against Carnigan's eyebrow trail.

Neither gorge yielded any signs of life. Carnigan began to worry.

He remained where he was, smoking three cigarettes, for a half an hour, then drank deeply from a nearby miniature rock tank, gathered up his butts carefully, put them into the pocket of his jacket, and, moving quietly, left the gorge.

At the mouth of the Reno canyon, he waited for one cigarette's time, checking the depths of the canyon so far as he could see it, and keeping a wary eye on the rimrock.

He was pretty certain that none of the followers would be able to get a horse up onto the ridges but an agile man could make it and look down on him.

He was almost certain that Reno and his band would have to wait for the stream to subside before they would leave the safe refuge.

The path up which he had brought the girl might be possible for a mountain sheep or even a really sure footed mountain mustang, but to try and force their horses up it would be a desperate venture. Even Carnigan, who knew it, had tried it only on foot and in desperation.

But the outlaws would be sure to lose at least one horse on the path, and none of them would risk being set afoot with the cavalry behind them and the Indians ranging the mountains.

There would be, he reckoned, a brisk argument in which Reno and Brinsley would try and persuade the others into accompanying them up the trail, and Natchez and Donner would refuse. They would favour the safer but slower route up the canyon.

Eventually, physical reality would intrude in favour of waiting. The stream which kept the outlaws in their cave and the cavalry from them would dwindle. When it subsided, both would move off.

The party in the cave would benefit first, so they would get away to an earlier start than the cavalry lower down.

But by now, the water must have gone down enough to let both get on the move.

He moved back again to his vantage point where he could see down both canyons, and made himself a capful of fire to cook some bacon strips. His coffee pot was halfway down Hand-me-Down now, so he made do with rainwater again.

The buckskin shirt with its long fringes had been stiffened in its drenching and drying, and he sat in his union suit, working it in his hands to make it supple once again, before he pulled it back on.

His long johns, he had to admit, were probably the better for their drenching. He longed for the clean clothes he had in the cabin, but they might as well have been on the moon.

The first Apache showed around mid-morning and Carnigan, watching him through the glasses, whistled between his teeth.

The man was large for an Apache, tall and rangy, on foot and as jumpy as a bug on a hot rock. Carnigan watched as he followed the tracks of the grulla, examined the place where he and the woman had rested, then stood up and looked down the shale slide down which she had departed.

The horse's progress was naturally easy to follow. The disturbed rock showed up sharply against the lighter colour of the rest of the slide, and the Apache followed it with his eyes and then started to cast around the rest of the area.

The man was not familiar to Carnigan, though there were plenty of Chiricahua Apaches he had neither seen nor met during his time with them. He wore a breech clout, desert moccasins and a turban of cloth around his head.

He turned to look up the hill and Carnigan was struck by the width of his face. Most Apaches tended to be square in the features, but this man's face was broader than it was deep. He was aged around thirty and had deeply recessed eyes.

Carnigan deliberately switched his gaze elsewhere and rested the glasses on the side of the canyon where he expected to see the bandits.

For some reason, a watched man can often feel that there are eyes upon him and this one was as jumpy as a sore tooth.

Down in the depths of the second canyon there was a flicker of movement, too. Carnigan grinned savagely. Strangely satisfying if the two parties of savages follow-

117

ing him should fall upon one another.

He checked on the Apache and found the man crouching, his eyes fixed on the mouth of the same gorge.

He had either heard the approaching horses, or seen the movement. At any rate, he remained where he was for a short period, and then turned and took a long, careful look up the hill at Carnigan's hiding place.

You clever bastard, Carnigan told him silently. Either you can feel me, smell me or see me. But you goddamn well know I'm here, don't you?

He changed the focus of his sight again, keeping the Apache in his peripheral vision, and almost missed the moment when the Indian slipped away down the canyon, presumably to warn his comrades.

Sure enough, within the next few minutes, first one and then another brown figure flickered into sight among the rocks. They had left their horses behind them, and hidden in the entrance to the defile up which the scalp hunters and, later, the cavalry, were now coming.

Carnigan smiled contentedly to himself, wished Reno and his friends no luck at all, and settled down to chew on a matchstick and watch the outcome of the battle.

Just to be on the safe side, though, he moved his vantage point along the side of the hill to a different cluster of boulders where he could get to the shale slide more quickly.

While the battle was at its height, he could make his way down the front of the slide to the pass and by the time it was all over, he would be half-way home.

He hoped.

He settled into his new fortress, put the Henry in the shade – in direct sunlight it would be too hot to handle in a half hour – and focused his field glasses on the mouth of the canyon.

Through the glasses the convection effect of the heat was exaggerated and the rocks swam and twisted in the lens. But he could recognize instantly the face which swam into focus.

Major Blake was sitting on his horse like a parade ground martinet, riding as though he was passing out at West Point.

Carnigan was so surprised that for a moment he was frozen.

Behind Blake came a trooper and behind him another. The man was leading his command into an ambush a four-year-old child could have warned him was waiting.

Carnigan swore long and bitterly but he had no choice. He reached for the loaded Henry, and drew an unwavering aim on a gap between rocks. There had been a gap between those two rocks when he had 'made friends with the earth' and that gap had been filled in with something dust coloured now.

The shot had an unexpectedly gratifying effect. The Apache who had been hiding there shot upright, and

119

Carnigan's next shot hit him in the chest and knocked him down again.

The Apache, caught by surprise, opened fire on the soldiers, but most of the troopers were still well down in the canyon, and invisible at least to Carnigan. Shouting within the rocks indicated they were deploying themselves.

Blake's horse went down and the soldier who had followed him into the open went off the back of his horse as though he had been axed. The horse ran on into the open.

There was a spatter of fire, and Carnigan saw Blake hopping from rock to rock as he rejoined his command. The major made it without obvious harm, and silence fell.

Carnigan took a moment to check the slopes above him and slapped a shot at a rock which had not been there earlier in the morning. The 'rock' flickered into action and vanished back into a cluster of boulders further away. A shot from below told Carnigan that his strong-point had been spotted, and he knew it also meant that warriors were on their way to lever him out of his commanding situation.

He was shifting his position to the foot of a rock which crouched in a little collection of scrubby bushes, and was veiled by a screen of cactus when there was a further outburst of shooting.

From the mouth of the canyon, a horseman burst into the open, flogging his mount on the uphill run.

Bullets raised puffs of dust from the rocks all

around him, but the horse, leaping wildly, eyes flaring madly, seemed immune to them.

The animal burst through the ring of Indians, knocking one racing figure out of its path and ran, belly down for the shale-slide.

As it came close to Carnigan's hideaway it ran out of luck. He heard the thump of the bullet, saw the little spurt of dust from its side, and the mount went down like a thrown stone, spilling the rider into the dust.

Behind it two Apaches came running and, as he saw the rider roll over and grab for his gun, Carnigan stood and pumped two slugs into the nearest of them.

The Indian's attention was on the fallen rider, or he would have dodged, but instead the .44 slugs took him in the breastbone, and knocked him on his back. So great was his momentum he even slid for a few inches before lying still.

Carnigan did not see him hit, because he was already aiming at the second Indian, but even as he worked the lever, the warrior was diving for cover and the shot was a clean miss.

It did give the fleeing rider a moment to dive over the rock into Carnigan's hideout, and filthy with dust and blood and panting hard.

It was Natchez.

Carnigan looked down at the Mexican with a mixture of surprise and disgust.

'I might have figured on you being the one to make a break for it, Sergeant Ruiz,' he said. 'You ran for it in that sweep in the San Antonios, too.'

Natchez grinned at him. 'I have change' my mind, *señor*,' he said. ' I report back for duty!'

A shot rattled into the rocks around them and both men ducked instinctively. For a while they were both busy returning a stinging searching fire from the Indians in the canyon and Carnigan knew it would be only a little time before other Apaches on the slopes could mount a dropping barrage into their refuge.

'They sure want you bad,' he remarked to Natchez during a lull. 'How come?'

'They recognize me, I theenk,' said Natchez. 'I was at Las Cruces two years ago and some of them got away. Ulzana was one.'

'Ulzana? He's out there?'

Natchez gave a grin in which there was much evidence of yellow teeth but no mirth.

'The beeg one is Ulzana. He has come a long way to find us, I theenk. A good hater, that one.'

Carnigan spat on the rock in front of him and took a long breath while he controlled his feelings.

Las Cruces had been one of the most recent and worst of the massacres of the Apache. A whole Apache *rancheria* had been wiped out in a day-long orgy of blood and cruelty. The final horror had come when the remaining men, women and children took refuge in a cave overlooking the smoking ruins of their homes in what should have been a safe haven in the hills.

The scalp hunters piled brushwood in front of the cave, set it on fire and smoked the refugees out. As they ran, choking, into the open, the guns were waiting for them.

Not one had survived that final horror – but unknown to the killers – there had been survivors among the piles of dead in the village itself. Ulzana had been one, and he became one of the most rabid of the Apache revenge-seekers.

Carnigan's Apache wife and child had not been among the survivors.

For a long moment he fought with the urge to tear Natchez's throat out on the spot. Then a bullet smacked off the rock in front of him and they were firing again, desperately hammering shots at the leaping, running figures in the rocks.

Over towards the mouth of the canyon, there was a spatter of firing, too.

How many of these hellions are there? Carnigan asked himself. When the battle had started he was counting on a dozen Indians at the most. But there had to be at least that number surrounding the two men now – and more keeping the soldiers pinned down.

'How did you come to be with Blake?' he asked Natchez. The Mexican squeezed off a shot at a dodging figure and missed.

'They overtook us in the canyon. We crossed over to this one, then the soldiers come. We had no chance to run until the Indians opened fire.'

Carnigan slid the Smith & Wesson down by his side where his hand would fall on it naturally.

'Still a liar, Ruiz. Reno wasn't handing over that gold to Blake and half a dozen shavetail soldiers without a fight. I'd a heard any shootin' down there this morning. What really happened?'

The Mexican grinned at him again, black eyes dancing.

'Always the *coronel*!' he said. 'No, they did not overtake all of us. They overtook only me.'

Carnigan rolled on his back and eased a cigarette out of the top pocket of his shirt, lighting it with a match flicked on his thumbnail.

'You better explain,' he said, puffing smoke.

Natchez removed his hat and there was a moment of tension as he fished inside, but all that emerged was a sadly damaged black cigar with a frayed end. He trimmed the end with his knife, and lit the cigar while he slipped the knife back into his boot.

A shot from the rocks buzzed over them as he blew out his plume of smoke and he laughed again.

'I do not of course trust this Reno,' he said comfortably. 'Once or twice, I see him watching me when he think I no look. I am of course a handsome man, *señor*, but not thees handsome. I begin to think that Reno see me as a share in his gold. I theenk I am a share he would like for himself.'

Irrelevantly, Carnigan noticed how the man's accent seemed stronger at some times than others. It was not unusual for a Mexican who spent more time in the company of Americans than his own countrymen, but in Natchez it seemed exaggerated. He found himself wondering if Natchez/Ruiz was in fact as Mexican as he seemed.

'Where do you come from, Ruiz?' he asked him suddenly.

'The north of Spain, *señor*. I am Basque,' Natchez told him simply. Carnigan nodded. He had met Basques before, survivors of the once independent state between France and Spain, now persecuted for their massive sense of independence.

There was even a small Basque settlement in California.

'So what happens now?'

'You finish tellin' me what brung you up here with Major Blake and his boys,' Carnigan told him, and suddenly the Apaches were upon them.

He shot one running figure in the chest and without waiting to see him fall, took another with his second shot. Then they were in the rocks, and he was shooting with the Smith & Wesson, hearing the yells and smelling the Apaches' frightening body smells.

There were three in the refuge with them, and Natchez cut down one with the butt of his rifle with a sweeping cavalry stroke which sank the stock into the man's head behind his temple.

Carnigan fired twice and missed, then jammed the muzzle into a brown belly and pulled the trigger. The Apache dropped as though his string had been cut, and then they were alone with the corpses.

Natchez eyed the fallen Indians expressionlessly.

'Dead, they look so small,' he said unexpectedly.

'You should be used to it by now,' Carnigan told him.

The Mexican shrugged. 'They are animals,' he said. 'But they fight like demons. Even the children.'

Carnigan found the cigarette he had dropped, and carefully relit it. He was getting short on tobacco and even more so on paper. Then, moving carefully so as not to expose himself, he pushed the corpses outside the circle of stones and as far away as he could get them. After a couple of hours in the sun they would stink badly.

'At least we know why they're this far north,' he said. The Mexican shot him a glance.

'They are looking for us,' he said simply. It was probably the first time he had spoken the truth since they had met.

Carnigan nodded. 'Ulzana would have run all this way on his bare feet to find you boys,' he said. 'And I happen to be with you.'

Natchez grinned. 'They pick up your tracks with ours, out at Antelope Rock, they will theenk you are one of us,' he agreed. 'Ees bad luck, this, *señor*!'

Carnigan agreed with him. Ulzana, as Natchez rightly said, was a good hater. Even among Apaches.

'Are all you boys out there with the Major?' he asked.

'No. I sneak away in the dawn. I am on watch, and they slept. I theenk it is a good time to go away. Black, Basque hair may look much the same as Apache to a scalp hunter.

'I find a cross-canyon and walk straight into the troopers. I tell them Reno is behind, but he no believe me. I don' know why not.'

'Hard to credit,' Carnigan agreed with him, sarcastically. ' I suppose you offered to lead him direct to the hideout?'

'Of course,' said Natchez. 'But he was no' interested. He theenks I am the rearguard and the others are up ahead.'

It was characteristic of Blake that the one time he was told the truth he chose not to believe it. Typical, too, that he would assume that because he himself would post a rearguard . . . even a bunch of outlaws would do the same.

Carnigan did not give much for the chances of a rearguard between Blake and Reno.

And now, here they were keeping the Apaches pinned down while Reno and his cohorts were escaping.

Carnigan realized with a start that while he was thinking, he had been absently watching a scrap of red rag which was being waved erratically over the top of a rock downhill to his front. He stared at it for a long moment, seeing it twitch and dance, then swore luridly and threw himself to one side, rolling frantically.

An Apache brave dropped into the space he had just left. Carnigan, still rolling, was caught with his gun-hand under him.

The Apache fired twice into Natchez' back, and spun

to fire at Carnigan, only to find him still moving away. For a moment he wavered, and Carnigan got his knife from his belt and threw it underhand into the man's chest. By chance, it missed the ribs and, travelling upwards, lanced into his heart. The Apache dropped.

Carnigan put a shoulder under him and levered him over the rock into the open. Instantly a bullet burned across the top of his shoulder. The rag which had been so successful in diverting his attention had disappeared now, but he bounced a bullet off the rock anyway, just to relieve his feelings.

Natchez was trying to push himself to his feet but his legs were lying lax and floppy. The two rifle bullets had passed through his body at point-blank range, breaking his spine and tearing out through his stomach. Carnigan sat back against the rock and looked at him.

'I been gut-shot,' said the outlaw unnecessarily. Carnigan nodded.

'I seen men who died from being gut-shot,' Natchez said. 'It is no' a good way to die.'

'There is no good way to die,' Carnigan told him.

'But some are quicker than others. Be merciful. I would be pleased if you would . . .'

'No,' said Carnigan, 'I won't. You see, I may not have been at Las Cruces, but my wife was. And our baby was. And they wasn't among the survivors.'

The faint hope faded from the Mexican's eyes.

'I see,' he said quietly. 'Nevertheless, I have my own gun and my knife.'

The shock which insulated him from the pain would wear off soon, both men knew. Natchez was not only mortally wounded, but also paralysed from the waist down. For the rest of his life, which could be counted in hours, maybe in minutes, he would know nothing but pain.

A rattle of hoofs and a spatter of shots diverted Carnigan's attention. To his amazement, accompanied by a chorus of derisive hoots, the Apaches were disappearing down Reno's canyon.

'What the hell?' He was turning back when he heard the sound behind him of a pistol being cocked. He threw himself over the rock in front to land almost upon the body of the Apache he had just killed.

Natchez fired in the same instant and the bullet puffed an angry spurt of powder from the top of the rock. Carnigan heard the man give a short, harsh laugh and another shot, strangely muffled.

He peered carefully round the rock and saw that Natchez had put the muzzle of his pistol into his mouth and pulled the trigger. The top of his head had been blown through the elaborate sombrero to stain the rock.

Cautiously,. Carnigan crossed the little plateau and met Blake and his men halfway. They were leading their horses and two of the men wore bandages. One – the man Carnigan had seen blown from his saddle – was tied face down across a led horse.

'Where is Miss Crawshaw?' Blake was at least consistent. He ignored the demands of the moment to chase issues which could easily have waited.

Carnigan eyed the horses angrily. Thanks to Blake's ridiculous entry to the plateau they were already two mounts short.

'I sent her to a safe place,' he said. 'What're you goin' to do with that trooper?'

'Take him down the mountain to a decent burial,' said Blake. 'Where is this place?'

Carnigan walked past him and examined the two bandaged men, then took a long look at the horses.

'You're two horses short a'ready,' he said, rolling himself one of his last cigarettes. 'You need that mount. Best thing you can do is bury him hereabouts and we'll read over him now. Don't make no never-mind to him, and we need his horse.'

'Two men can ride double,' said Blake stiffly. 'The regiment takes care of its own.'

Carnigan flicked a match on his fingernail and gave the officer a narrow stare.

'I see you're not goin' to be one of them ridin' double,' he said quietly. 'And the regiment'd be better lookin' after its live troopers than trailin' a dead one round the goddam' mountain.'

Blake flushed,

'Now you see here . . .' he began.

'No,' said Carnigan. 'You see here. Them Injuns gone off in a rush like that for a good reason.'

'We drove them off!' protested Blake.

'No, Major, you didn't drive 'em off. You wasn't even irritatin' them. They simply found somethin'

130

they rather do than swap lead with you. That's what drove 'em off. Now, there's two things an Apache wants more than your hair. There's Reno, Brinsley and Donner, and there's Miss Crawshaw.'

The officer looked sick.

'Now, I don't reckon they know about Miss Crawshaw yet. So what they gone after was them scalp hunters, and they goin' to be right busy with them for a while, 'cause first they got to catch them, then they got to fry 'em. Then, they're goin' to go off a-lookin' for Miss Crawshaw.'

Blake opened his mouth to argue again but Carnigan was relentless.

'Now, you're just about to ask me how they'll know about Miss Crawshaw and I'm goin' to tell you it's because Reno, Brinsley and Donner'll tell 'em. By the time those Apache is through with that crowd they'll tell them anything they know to make them stop and Miss Crawshaw is an obvious one.

'They'll say she's with you, because that's where they think she is by this time, so sometime tomorrow them Apache are goin' to come lookin' for you again.

'By that time, we got to be where I sent her because that's the best place to fort-up around here. And we've got to get there almighty fast, 'cause everything I just said is just guesswork, and they may just beat us to it.'

EIGHT

Carnigan's guesswork had been right about one thing. The Apache had been called away about more urgent business. That business was Mart Donner and he was about at the end of his tether.

When Reno and his men awakened in the glory of the mountain morning to find that Natchez had deserted them, the leader spent several minutes cursing the absent sentry and then assembled men, money and mounts in the cave mouth.

'By this time,' he said, 'Natchez has gone up the trail. We'll try going over the mountain. If that bastard Carnigan can do it in the dark, I'm damn sure we can do it in the light. Mart, I'll let you lead out and I'll ride drag. Leave a gap between yourselves.'

Brinsley gave him a slantendicular look, but raised no objection. Donner led out, his shotgun balanced across his knees. Brinsley gave him a short interval, and Reno watched first one and then the other wind

132

his way up the faint trail over the shoulder of the mountain and out of sight.

Then he mounted his horse and descended to the floor of the gorge where he searched in the wet mud for tracks. He found them almost instantly, and they told him the cavalry troop had already passed that way. The way down the mountain was therefore open.

By the time Brinsley and Donner realized that both their gold and their leader were missing, it was far too late for them to retrace their tracks to find him, even if either had been inclined the take the risk on a trail which was little more than a scratch in a boulder suspended over space.

Donner cursed in a steady stream of filth which exasperated Brinsley, who merely looked puffed with poison and spat tobacco juice on a nearby rock.

'He's been plannin' this all along,' Brinsley said when Donner paused for lack of breath and invention. 'Iffen he didn't get a chance to drop us, he'd a poisoned the coffee, or slit our throats in the night. Be glad you still got your breath.'

Donner fell silent for a while, during which a second thought crossed his mind.

'He sent us over the ridge on account of this is where he thinks the Injuns are at!' he said suddenly. Brinsley shook his head.

'We on'y got Carnigan's word they was any Apache on this mountain in the first place,' he said. 'Powerful far north for a 'pache, specially a Chiricahua. I reckon that was just to keep us quiet where we was. Git a move on, Mart, and we'll top out before noon.'

In fact it was a little after noon when they arrived on top of the ridge where Carnigan and the woman had rested. They chose almost exactly the same place for their nooning.

'I bin thinkin',' said Brinsley, sipping his coffee.

Donner gave him a dark look.

'Sounds like trouble,' he muttered.

Brinsley rolled a cigarette and stared out over the landscape. It was a sight of breathtaking beauty with the reddish dun of the rocks at this height giving way to the dark masses of trees on the slopes below and in the distance the marching masses of the snow-covered peaks. But Donner surveyed it without seeing its beauty.

'I reckon Reno's headin' for Hand-me-Down Pass,' said Brinsley. 'Not far down there, the ground levels out a mite, and you can ride through the trees across to where Hand-me-Down comes out above Placerville. Iffen he goes that way, he can be up Hand-me-Down and over the mountain by tomorrow night. He'll be free, clear and rich, and we'll still be up here with the goddamn military!'

Donner considered the idea for a while, then nodded.

'So?'

'So we cut across here and meet him comin' up. Won't be no trick at all, iffen he goes down into the trees. Must be all o' twenty miles across to the mouth of Hand-me-Down. Then he's got to come up 'er again. We cross these two ridges and we can be there afore him!'

Donner gestured at the bones of the mountain standing out before them.

'Cross over there? Yo're funnin'!'

Brinsley was not to be denied.

'No, I ain't! Just because it ain't bin done don't mean it cain't be done. Look.' He hunkered down and drew a rough map in the soil caught in a bowl in the rocks. The heat of the sun had already started turning it from mud back into dust, despite their altitude.

'We're here, atop this ridge. All we have to do is go down this canyon, cross over her and move up about a mile or so. There's a place there.' He pointed and Donner stood up with him and looked. 'A place we can get the horses up, I reckon.'

From here it looked a possibility, and Donner could find no fault with the plan.

It also occurred to him that he was riding a mountain-bred horse whose footing was sure as any sheep. Brinsley's mount, though bigger, was not as sure-footed.

The more he thought about it, the better the idea seemed to him. When they had finished their break and watered their horses with a drink poured into their hats, they moved out.

They were already in the gut of the canyon when they heard the pattering of shots from above that signalled the opening of the battle between the army patrol and the Indians.

135

For a moment they considered running for it down the mountain. Then they realized that the intensity of shooting was such that a static fight was taking place.

'While they are thinkin' about old Blake and his soldier-boys, they won't be worryin' about us,' opined Brinsley. 'We'd best push on.'

Neither man expressed surprise that there were obviously Indians on the mountain, despite their earlier conversation. The Army could not be fighting anyone else.

Donner led the way into a cleft in the rocks which they had seen from the far ridge. But they had not gone very far into it when it became apparent that Brinsley's heavier horse was not up to the task of the climb. Donner's, on the other hand, breasted the slope readily, planting its feet like a tightrope walker and turning its head from the drop.

Brinsley fell back a little, and then a lot. After a while his horse refused to go on, and he sat watching while Donner's back disappeared round a bend in the rock wall.

There was enough room – just – for his horse to turn round on the trail, and Brinsley was a superb horseman.

He managed to turn the horse and ride it back down the trail into the canyon. There he dismounted and rolled himself a smoke while he considered his next move.

He would have been better advised to turn that magnificent horse and ride for his life.

Before Ulzana had taken the main body of his warriors up the canyon to head off Major Blake and the man they all knew as Natchez, he had left two sentries where the trail came over the ridge.

One man was to watch for travellers. The other to carry word of what they saw.

The two watched until Brinsley and Donner had topped out on the rock and come down into the canyon. By the time they started up the other side, the runner was already on his way to bring Ulzana back. The other, a cautious man, had already ascended the trail up which Donner now urged his mountain horse.

He sat at the top, his rifle across his knees, and watched with interest as Donner picked his way up the face of the cliff.

The Apache had been trained in the hardest school in the world. Added to which he had lived every day of his life in the knowledge that something or someone was continually trying to kill him.

All of this he looked upon, if he considered it at all, as unremarkable. Any man capable of less he considered less than an animal. His only word for 'stranger' also meant 'enemy'.

A hoof rattled on the rock, and the Indian leaned forward to look over the edge of his rocky platform at the ascending rider.

The man was hunched over the horse's neck, trying

to get his weight as far forward on the animal as possible.

It was important to take the scalp hunter alive. The mercy of a quick bullet would be poor recompense for the suffering of the Apache women and children who had died because of these men.

Besides, it would be important to find out how brave they were.

As Mart Donner topped out on the narrow trail, the Apache rose to his feet, the first movement he had made since the rider came into direct line of sight.

The horse had not seen the Indian as it came up the trail and to man and animal it was as though the warrior had grown out of the bare rock. He spooked the horse, and it reared up and took two tiny steps sideways.

Donner, who had been looking behind him to see what had happened to Brinsley, was caught unawares. He made a wild grab at the saddle horn, missed and fell backwards out of the saddle.

His boot caught in the stirrup and instead of pitching down the drop into the canyon, he fell sideways against the canyon wall where a jagged cleft ran down into the side of the face.

The boot came off his left foot, and he fell head down some six feet into the crack until the narrowing walls held him alive, but immobile, above the drop.

The Apache took the reins of the frightened horse, and calmed it, then leaned over the drop to see his quarry wriggling, but firmly jammed, hanging head down below him.

Satisfied that the man was not going to escape, he settled down to examine the contents of the saddle-bags.

The first thing he found was Donner's collection of scalps, and he laid them out one by one on the rock in front of him. There were twenty-three of them. Ten were very small, and the Apache looked at them with eyes like stone for some time.

Trapped in the cleft, Mart Donner could reach his gun but not get it from its holster. He was facing outward and before his eyes he could see, upside down, the floor of the canyon. By swivelling his eyes – for his head was held fast – he could see the first of the Apaches coming down the pass. He could also see Brinsley, riding as fast as he could go for the foot of the canyon.

A scraping from above made him shift his hand on the Colt but he could still neither draw nor aim the weapon.

Some small stones fell past his face and he heard the Indian above grunt as he moved his position. Then something fell on his exposed foot and he screamed with pain. It was burning and though he kicked again and again, he could not dislodge it.

The Apache stood up and waved to Ulzana as he arrived at the foot of the trail. A swift patter of sign language conveyed that there was a prisoner and where he was. Ulzana considered the trail, then dismounted and made his way up on foot.

'Where is he?' he asked as he arrived at the top. The

139

watchman led him to the crack and demonstrated. He also showed the collection of scalps taken from the saddle-bags.

Ulzana, too, stared at them for a long time. Then he squatted down and conferred with his watchman.

Strictly speaking the watchman was not a warrior at all. He was a medicine man of the Mimbres Apache and a mystic who saw visions, which was why his advice was always sought.

He was also a healthy hater which Ulzana respected, and a man with a rich vein of invention when it came to the inflicting of pain.

They talked together for a short time, paying occasional visits to the cleft to drop burning embers from their fire onto Donner's feet and clothing. When they did so, the watchers in the canyon responded with enthusiastic yells.

Then the medicine man pointed out that the rock shaft was admirably adapted as a chimney, and that the lower end was easily accessible from the trail.

Ulzana sent men to collect kindling and some green branches from the scrubby mountain pines. He did not want a fire which become too hot too quickly.

The medicine man left him to the mechanics of the operation while he attended to certain spiritual aspects of the treatment of the original owners of the scalps and their after-life.

But for the rest of his life, he never forgot the hair of the children on the rock, nor its significance.

His name was Geronimo.

NINE

Reno behaved exactly as Brinsley had predicted, but even Brinsley could not have foreseen the pure dumb luck which brought him to the bald knob in Hand-me-Down Pass in time to see the tracks of the grulla horse leading into the little hanging valley.

He was aware he needed a place to hide. Sound travels well, if quirkily, in the mountains and the funnelling valley had brought the popping of the fight on the plateau to him as he rounded out from the gorge and started to traverse the mountainside.

By pushing his horse unmercifully, he brought the animal nearly halfway up Hand-me-Down Pass and was passing the knob of rock when he saw the tracks of the mouse-coloured horse ascending.

He followed the tracks for a while, in the hope of stealing himself another horse, before it occurred to him that the rider was aiming for the notch in the rim of the pass, and his pace quickened to catch up.

Marion Crawshaw was already in the valley

Carnigan called his 'claim' when Reno entered the notch on the rim of the pass.

It was late afternoon, but Reno had almost caught up with her when she reached the cabin, and dazzled by the beauty of the valley, stopped to rest.

It was a stunning place.

Trees lined the sides of the valley and the crags which bordered the lake. Above towered mountains glaring white in the afternoon sun. There was a plume of snow blowing from a peak over the valley, white as smoke against the deep, deep blue of the sky.

The cabin itself was tucked back on a bench of turf to one side of the feather of water which fell with a muted thunder into a rocky channel leading to the lake. The house was of trimmed logs on a base of stones taken from the meadow before it. To one side, there was a stable and a large corral. On the meadows near the lake, cattle grazed and there were horses.

Wondering at the loveliness of the place, she let the grulla make its own way across the grass towards the house.

Behind her, Reno came from the trees and urged his tired horse into a trot to catch up with her.

Carnigan, Blake, and the now-depleted command, made their way on tiring horses to Hand-me-Down.

Timms, one of the wounded men, was in great pain from a bullet which had glanced off a rock and lodged against his hip, distorted and jagged. Twice they had to stop to dress his wound again.

'If we don't stop and let him rest, he'll bleed to death. He's losing too much blood,' Blake acknowledged to Carnigan after the second stop.

The scout nodded. 'If we leave him and Ulzana comes down this way, he'll lose all of it,' he said grimly. Blake had to agree with his judgement.

'What can we do with him?'

Carnigan pointed to the knob of rock towering over the pass.

'On this side o' that knob, there's a hanging valley,' he said. 'Take the patrol up there, and along the valley behind it, until you come to a basin with a lake. Across the lake is a cabin. It's my place and we can bed him down there and nurse him.'

'What if the Apache catch up?'

'Then they ain't goin' to be as many of 'em goin' home as there was come out a-lookin',' the scout said flatly. 'I done run enough these last few days. Now, I'm gettin' kind o' mad. I'll see you there.'

He set off at a fast canter and the patrol, strung out along the bottom of the pass, followed him at a more sober pace. Blake, now that he knew where Carnigan was going, led them up the side of the pass towards the notch in the skyline.

Brinsley watched the patrol coming towards him from a boulder on the side of the bald knob. Behind him, his horse snuffled into the bandanna he had bound over its nostrils, and he held his hand firmly over its mouth in case it should whicker and betray him.

Despite all his efforts, though, the horse remained restless while he watched the line of tiny figures climb the side of the pass and disappear into the shallow notch above.

It was only when the soldiers had finally vanished and the horse's agitation had failed to abate that it occurred to him there might be another reason for its restiveness.

He looked round into the flat, obsidian, eyes of Ulzana.

Carnigan cantered the tired horse along the valley and out into the basin he thought of as home.

His horses and cattle grazed peacefully enough, and there was the grulla in the corral near the cabin. All seemed well.

He started the borrowed cavalry mount towards the cabin, walking easily, and allowed himself to relax a whisker of his vigilance while he watched the reflection of the mountains in the lake surface.

A tiny flicker of unease ruffled his mind when Marion did not appear on the porch at his approach. He had expected her to be keeping an eye open for him at least, if not also for the enemy. She had much to lose.

When he was within a hundred yards of the building, he pulled up the horse and rose in the stirrups to survey the building more closely. It looked serene enough. The shutters were in place, the door closed and the whole outfit looked just as he had left it.

He still did not feel comfortable. Was he riding into

a trap? Marion must be here because the horse was. So why did she not show herself?

He rode in a long arc towards the stable, from which he could approach the house more obliquely.

He had designed the place as a miniature fort, without blind spots, and with a clear field of fire across the yard.

Perhaps she was asleep. He put his hand to his mouth to call out, but as he did so, the door opened and the girl appeared on the porch.

'Marion!' he said, relieved. But the rigid way she was standing warned him all was not right. As he began to step out of the saddle, a horse whickered from the stable and he knew they had trouble.

The soldiers were not even in sight across the basin yet. If Marion was being held under the gun by somebody inside the house, there was no way Carnigan could get in a shot without the girl being forfeit.

Marion turned her head slowly and looked along the porch towards him.

'Carnigan?' she said in a strained voice.

'Yo!'

'You are to drop your gun and walk round to the front of the house where Reno can see you.'

He completed his dismount on the far side of the horse. If he dropped his guns now both he and the girl were dead. Reno would kill him immediately, and the girl later when he had done with her.

Reno did not yet know that the army was only a little way behind Carnigan. There was a serious danger that

145

when they did emerge from the trees behind, the sight might panic him into murdering the two by the cabin anyway and making for the trail by the waterfall.

Either way, Carnigan and the woman he was supposed to be protecting would be dead.

Leading the horse and keeping it carefully between him and the doorway, Carnigan walked to the front of the cabin.

'Tell him to come out where I can see him!' he said to the woman.

She was white to the lips.

'Carnigan, run for it!' she said suddenly. 'Ride, now! He'll kill us both!'

From within the house, Reno shouted explosively: 'You better believe it, Carnigan! But you'll both live longer if you drop the gun. Maybe I'll let her live, afterwards!'

'Come out on the stoop!' Carnigan shouted. 'Make like you're a man for once!'

There was a snigger from the darkness within the doorway. Carnigan itched with frustration. He had designed and built that doorway himself, and he knew that a man could stand within it and be sheltered by thick logs from incoming fire. There was no way of getting at Reno without first getting him outside the door.

'You ain't got much time, Reno,' he told the outlaw. 'Blake's follerin' me down with the soldiers. I come ahead to see Miss Crawshaw was all right. They'll be here in a few minutes.'

146

'Then I better get on with it, hadn't I?' The voice was taunting but there was an undercurrent of rage in it. Reno was used to being the planner, the controller, the manipulator. Now he was out of control and being pushed towards action he had not planned.

'Come on out, Reno,' Carnigan called in a voice he allowed to sound weary. 'All you got to do is down me, and you're free and clear. You can take the horse, and go up the trail by the waterfall before the soldiers come. Here, you're in a trap. Yo're runnin' out of time, Blake's on his way and Ulzana's out there in the hills lookin' for you. You need all the runnin' time you can get.'

The gunman was silent. Carnigan, tuned up to the tightest tension, could almost hear his frustration. Inside the cabin Reno had been secure until now. But he must know he could not hold it against a determined attack by trained troops.

Reno was sure that Carnigan spoke the truth when he mentioned Ulzana. He had heard that the Apache was in the San Juans on a vengeance hunt, raiding as he went. He was also pretty certain that the same group of Apache who were now, uncharacteristically, in the Uncompahgres were Ulzana's band and if so, that he and his associates were their quarry.

The trouble was that he could not get a clear shot at Carnigan from where he stood. He could see past the girl's slim figure to where the horse stood in the early evening sunlight. Carnigan's legs, though, were behind the horse's legs, his body behind its shoulder.

147

If Reno stepped out on to the porch he gave up his advantage of invisibility to the scout.

At this moment, Marion Crawshaw resolved the situation quite simply.

Calmly and without fuss, she stepped off the porch and walked in two steps out of Reno's field of vision.

The act was done in such a matter of fact fashion that for a split second neither man registered it.

Then Carnigan levered the action of the Henry and fired into the darkness inside the door. The bullet burned across the outside of Reno's left arm, opening a bloody groove which bled profusely.

The shot crossed with Reno's own first round, which hit the standing horse in the neck and caused it to go bucking across the yard, knocking Carnigan flat on his back and kicking the Henry away from his grasp.

Reno stepped out on to the stoop at last, firing downwards at Carnigan who was an indistinct figure, rolling desperately in the dust.

Carnigan rolled and rolled again, then catapulted to his feet, grabbing for his pistol.

Reno followed the moving figure with his foresight, thumbing back the hammer of the Colt. This time, he knew, it would be the killing shot. This time, he had Carnigan full to rights.

'I got you, you bastard!' he cried.

But in a world which seemed suddenly to have slowed to unreality, Carnigan was coming to his feet, a gun in his hand.

Reno felt his own finger tighten on the trigger with nightmare slowness. But the aim was true. The gun hammered into his hand just as the girl screamed like a steam whistle in his ear.

The shot was a clean miss, but the next one would be the killer, he knew.

As his finger tightened, Reno felt something hit him with terrible force in the face. It felt as though a horse had kicked him and for a split second he thought the girl had struck him with a weapon.

But he saw the gun in Carnigan's hand, and he saw the flame flicker in its muzzle. There was smoke hanging in the yard.

He never actually felt the bullet which shattered his brain, but in the last fraction of a second of life, he knew what had happened to him.

He did not believe it.

Blake and his cavalry arrived in the yard to find Carnigan standing over the body, his Smith & Wesson still smoking, and the black powder haze still hanging in the calm, evening air.

They came from the trees beyond the lake strung out in a skirmish line, guns in hand, and scattered the horses and cattle as they rode through them, even wounded Trooper Timms sitting upright, a cocked Colt in his right fist.

Carnigan reloaded the Smith & Wesson and dropped it into his holster, then picked up the Henry and used it to despatch the wounded cavalry horse, which was bleeding to death by the corral.

'Tell me,' he asked Blake as the officer dismounted with fine style from his horse. 'Why is it the goddam' cavalry only arrives in the nick o' time in them dime noveletties?'

Blake eyed him balefully. He, too, had gone through a full and harrowing day and he was heartily sick of being in the wrong.

'If you have any complaints about my command, Carnigan—'

'Major,' said Carnigan, 'if I was to list the complaints I got about yore command, we'd still be standing here talkin' when the Indians arrive, so we ain't got time.'

'Indians?' Blake spun in time to see Ulzana and his band burst out of the trees and race towards the lake.

'Two men in the stable with the horses, the rest in the cabin!' bellowed Blake. Here was a situation he was trained for, and his instincts fired him into action.

As the soldiers ran for their positions, Carnigan turned, picked up Marion Crawshaw with one arm around her waist, and threw her through the open door of the cabin. He heard a shrill gasp as she fell against something, and then he was inside as well.

He put his eye and the Henry to the loophole in one shutter.

Ulzana and his men spread into a line as they came up from the lake, and for a moment Carnigan thought they were simply going to charge the waiting guns, but at the last moment, barely within range, they split up and peeled away to either side.

They were too far away for effective shooting, though there was a shot from the stable before Blake roared: 'Hold your fire!

'Got any ammunition?' he asked Carnigan, and the scout nodded and pointed to a shelf by the fireplace. One of the troopers broke open boxes and shared the rounds out to the waiting troopers.

The Indians came together in a bunch out of range. Carnigan noticed that two of the horses remained apart from the rest, he peered through the deepening dusk. He gave a low whistle.

'What is it?' asked Blake.

'Cain't swear to it, but I reckon that's Brinsley,' Carnigan told him. 'You got any glasses?'

Blake had, but they were on his saddle and his saddle was on his horse in the stable. Carnigan clucked testily, and did his best with a rolled up bit of bark from the fireplace. It concentrated the attention.

The light was failing, but he could make out the sloping shoulders and the broken-down hat which had become familiar to him. The scalp hunter was tied to his horse, which was being led by a warrior.

'Major!' One of the look-outs was pointing, and Carnigan saw one Apache urge his horse forward, riding at a walk. He was a tall, well built man for an Apache, and he carried a lance.

When he reached a point halfway between the

Indians and the cabin, he reined in, and plunged the lance into the ground, point down.

'What's he up to?' asked Blake.

'Wants to talk,' said Carnigan. 'You want to go make powwow with him?'

He grinned at the uncertainty on Blake's face and handed him the Henry.

'Don't worry, Major. It's me he wants to talk to.'

He opened the door and stepped on to the stoop in the dusk. Above their heads, the peaks were red with the dying sunlight, and the reflection threw an eerie copper light into the valley.

Carnigan slipped the thong from his gun, and walked slowly across the yard to where the Indian sat on his pony. He had no illusions about the Indian's sense of honour. If Ulzana found it expedient to kill him, he would do so without a thought. The lance, point down in the ground, did not count for anything.

But he was determined that if he was to die, he would not die alone.

He was, however, still counting on the fact that the Apache did not know Marion Crawshaw was inside, or, being inside, that she was a woman.

He was surprised, too, to see how few warriors remained in the band. He assumed that it had split during the day and wondered where the others were. Donner could have told him.

Ulzana looked down at him from the horse. His face had no more expression than the mountain above.

152

'Speak,' he said.

'You're the one wanted to talk. Talk!' Carnigan told him.

'Give me the man called Reno,' said Ulzana in Spanish. 'I have come for him.'

'You came too late,' Carnigan told him in his own language. 'He is dead.'

'Show me.'

Carnigan nodded, gestured him towards the corpse, and stood back while the Indian slipped from the horse and turned the body over. The two fat slugs of lead had destroyed the back of the head, but there was enough of the face left to see who it had been.

'He died too quick,' said Ulzana, and he leaned over and spat deliberately into what was left of the face. Then he jumped back on his horse and turned it away.

Wary as a cat, Carnigan stayed where he was, his hand almost touching his gun.

Ulzana turned his horse away, and rode several yards before he turned to look over his shoulder.

'You were at Las Cruces?' he asked. Carnigan shook his head.

'My wife and my baby were at Las Cruces,' he said. 'They were killed there. That is why I took Reno for myself.'

The Indian nodded.

'They said you were Walks Long,' he said. 'I did not believe it. I said Walks Long would not have been with the killers. Now I see that it is true. But I also see the reason, and it is good.'

153

'Where will you go now?' Carnigan asked him, moved by a sudden curiosity as well as anxiety to make sure Ulzana was on his way south again.

The Indian grunted.

'I will return to my people,' he said. 'I have a gift for them for which they have waited a long time.'

He pulled the lance from the ground and waved it above his head, then kicked the pony into motion. As he approached the group of warriors he shouted to them, and there was a chorus of yells. Then, to Carnigan's enormous relief, the whole group turned their horses and rode away across the meadow.

He noticed even in the growing gloom that the figure tied to the horse was wriggling madly, and even his experience-hardened stomach rolled queasily as he realised what Ulzana's gift for his people would be.

'The trouble with ridin' the outlaw trail,' he told the dead horse as he tramped past it across his own back yard to face the major's incredulous barrage of questions, 'is that you meet such a goddam' unpleasant bunch of people!'

TEN

He rode with the soldiers to the mouth of the hanging valley the following morning and saw them start down the pass towards Placerville and the Army. Blake, who had now recovered both his charge, and the gold, unbent enough to snap a stiff salute before he turned away. The woman hung back.

'What will you do now?' she asked him. She was wearing clean fresh jeans and shirt from Carnigan's own stock, and riding astride a horse she had picked out of his herd. She looked as pretty as paint, and clean-cut as the mountains.

'Settle down and raise horses. Might even get myself a family,' he said. 'I seen a great deal o' the world and it seemed to me the guys with their own place and growin' kids had a mighty satisfied look, even when they wasn't rich.

'Travel's fun. But a man should have roots and that's the only way this country is goin' to amount to anythin', when people like me start puttin' in foundations and buildin' chimneys.'

'You believe in this country, then?'

'Should. I fought long enough for it.'

'You have been in the army, then?'

'Bin in three. The British army in India, this 'un, and the Mexican. And in one or two you wouldn't rightly call armies.'

She considered him gravely through deep violet eyes.

'You should meet my father,' she said. 'You would have a lot to talk about, you know. In many ways you are very alike. Why don't you come and visit us at the Fort next time you're down in Placerville?'

'Maybe I will,' he said.

'I shall count on it,' she said seriously. Then, with apparent irrelevance: 'Tell me, Carnigan, do you believe in big families?'

Suddenly Carnigan realized that maybe Apache Indians were not after all the greatest hazard a man had to face in the mountains.

ER

G15